"You're a goo[d...]
Dr. Bannin[g...]

He stood close enou[gh...] warmth of his body and smell the faint aroma of some wonderful after-shave with a woody flavor. She came to his chin, which she noted was aggressively firm but displayed a slight hint of a cleft.

Since graduation she'd dated a couple of men from work, nothing serious. Dinner and a movie. None of them compared to Jarod Banning. In fact, she'd never met anyone like him. For want of a better word, he seemed complete. A total man. One in whom she had inherent trust.

She took a deep breath. His strong, steady hand reached out and cupped her chin.

"You're a fighter, Kit, and that means everything," he said with intense feeling, yet sounding very far away. Then his hand dropped.

Dear Reader,

From an early age I loved boys and always thought they were a lot more fun than girls. My first official date with a boy was in grade school. His name was Dix. We were both ten years old. His mother picked me up in their Chrysler and drove us to an Esther Williams movie called *Neptune's Daughter*. His mother sat four rows behind us at the theater. I was in heaven.

When I look back on that experience, I chuckle. Yet interestingly enough, the years have only increased my love of the male gender. Somewhere around the age of fourteen or fifteen I read Anya Seton's book, *Katherine*, and fell head over heels in love with John of Gaunt, the fascinating, thrilling, famous English Duke of Lancaster. He became my hero, and I've been looking for him ever since.

After I finished my book *Kit and the Cowboy*, I realized that, after all these years of holding out for a hero, I'd found him in the guise of one Jarod Banning. Jarod is a hero Kit finds every bit as fascinating, thrilling, exciting, passionate and, yes, *perfect,* as the medieval duke who took possession of my young girl's heart.

If you've never been in love, or even if you have, prepare yourself to fall for this hero. He's the stuff a young maid or modern woman's dreams are made of.

Happy reading!

Rebecca Winters

Some men are worth waiting for!

Kit and the Cowboy
Rebecca Winters

Harlequin Books

TORONTO • NEW YORK • LONDON
AMSTERDAM • PARIS • SYDNEY • HAMBURG
STOCKHOLM • ATHENS • TOKYO • MILAN
MADRID • WARSAW • BUDAPEST • AUCKLAND

To my wonderful, brilliant, lovely daughter-in-law, Lori,
who has made my son's life complete.

ISBN 0-373-03419-9

KIT AND THE COWBOY

First North American Publication 1996.

Copyright © 1996 by Rebecca Winters.

CHAPTER ONE

"SHE'S bleeding, but refused to let me drive her to the hospital. I figured you'd take a look since you've handled other charity cases in the neighborhood after dark. Hell, if she were my daughter, I wouldn't let her go home alone after a performance. Not when it's downtown Salt Lake."

"She's not exactly a teenager, and more likely than not she knows her way around."

Kit bristled at the second man's comment, but the pain in her head prevented her from remonstrating. Besides—only one thing mattered. *She was safe!*

Elation washed over her and she closed her eyes, enjoying the warmth of the room after the freezing cold January night outside. Despite her fall on the ice, she experienced a sense of well-being because she'd outwitted her pursuer. He could be frantically searching the faces of the crowd this very minute, unable to find her.

Tonight, all traces of Kit Mitchell had vanished. Now that she'd made it this far, she had no intention of going back to her former life. In a few days, when she'd worked out a plan, she'd contact her sister, Laura, to let her know she was alive and well. Right now she needed to savor this feeling of safety.

Ever since the investigating officer suggested that the man sending her threatening notes probably knew her well, Kit had considered the idea of running away. She couldn't trust any of her friends or acquaintances. Worse, she'd been forced to suspect her co-workers at the office. Fear had brought her to the breaking point.

When she felt the edges of the purple satin cape she'd thrown on at the last minute being pulled away from her body, Kit's eyes flew open.

A tall man with a powerful physique stood over her, casually dressed in Levi's and a blue T-shirt that matched his eyes—their color the intense blue of Lake Tahoe where her family had always vacationed until her parents' deaths.

Brown eyebrows, unusually well shaped for a man, marked his incredible eyes. Beneath the glare of the overhead light, his brown hair glinted with unmistakable gold highlights. He needed a shave.

"Well, what have we here?" His firm, well-cut mouth displayed a ghost of a smile. "A real live swan on my hands and looking wounded to her very heart."

His penetrating eyes left her face and traveled over the rest of her, his expression revealing nothing as he examined the swelling high on her forehead, running into her hairline.

Kit felt his fingers at her throat, touching its hollow and the area behind her ears and below her jaws. The man was a doctor, obviously, and the examination purely professional. But his touch made her jerk nervously as he pulled off the white headdress with its dramatic widow's peak, revealing her short, silky black hair.

He slid his hand through the glistening strands to the base of her skull, apparently assuring himself she had no other head injuries. "Where else do you hurt?"

Kit blinked. "When I felt myself falling, I put out my hand. It feels like I burned it. Otherwise, I'm all right."

One eyebrow quirked as he examined the superficial scrape on her palm, then took her blood pressure.

She tried to pull away. "This isn't necessary."

"I'll be the judge of that," he said mildly, but she heard the unmistakable ring of authority. After he'd unfastened the arm cuff, he said, "Your pressure is a little high and your pulse is too fast for my liking. Are you always this jerky and tense?"

"Only after a fall."

But her sarcasm seemed to have no effect on him because he said, "The accident might have produced some trauma, but I have the feeling you've been living on the edge of your nerves for a long time."

The man was psychic.

He reached for his stethoscope and placed it against her chest. Gently helping her to a sitting position, he listened to her lungs from the back. "They're clear." He eased her back down on the bed.

"Please—" Kit tried to get up again, but he put his hands against her shoulders to prevent movement ''—I'm feeling much better. Is this examination necessary?''

He ignored her while he cleansed the lump on her forehead. ''I'm almost through,'' he assured her and applied a sterile gauze bandage. After taking another pulse reading, he tended to the scrape on her hand.

''There's nothing wrong with me,'' she asserted. But she'd seen herself in a mirror earlier and knew the heavy makeup exaggerated the forlorn, lost look on her face. It caused her gray-green eyes to appear haunted and larger than normal.

''Not physically, perhaps,'' he muttered while using a special light to examine her eyes, nose and throat.

Kit had to keep quiet while he took her temperature, but his astute observation unnerved her. It seemed an eternity before he told her she could get up and use the bathroom to remove her makeup, if she felt steady enough.

''There's lotion in the cabinet. While you're doing that, I'll bring you something to wear.''

She swung her legs slowly over the side of the bed and, with his assistance, rose to her feet. To her relief, the dizziness was subsiding.

''All right?'' he inquired, still holding her arm.

''Yes. I'm not as light-headed.''

''Good. You've suffered a mild concussion, but you seem to have recovered sufficiently to be mobile. I won't give you anything for pain tonight in case it should mask something more serious. If by morning you have no complications, but the pain is worse, I'll give you some tablets.''

"I don't plan to be here in the morning, Dr...."

"Banning. Jarod Banning. Internal medicine."

When she noted the closed expression on his face, she moistened her lips. "If you'd call me a taxi, I'll be on my way." She'd go to the Salvation Army tonight. "Here." She pulled a five-dollar bill from the bodice of the swan costume. "I'll pay you the remainder when I can."

He stood next to the bed with his arms folded, ignoring her outstretched hand. "When was the last time you ate? I'd estimate you're a good ten pounds underweight."

His doctor's eye didn't miss a trick. Since she'd started finding those terrifying notes, her life had become a living nightmare. Food was anathema to her. "I had breakfast," she lied.

"A cup of coffee, maybe," he said in disgust. "You need to eat to keep up your strength."

"I'm grateful for your help, but I'm no longer your concern, Dr. Banning. I was only dazed and now I feel fine."

Kit reached for her cape and started to put it around her shoulders, but a sudden weakness made her hands tremble as she tried to fasten the snap.

His keen eyes swept over her. "How far do you think you'll get in your condition? No shoes, no proper clothes? Certainly a place like the shelter or the Salvation Army isn't an answer," he said, reading her mind clearly. "Under the circumstances, you're asking for a different kind of trouble if you go out in the snow dressed in feathers.''

Her heart pounded. ''What are you implying?''

''Exactly what you think I'm implying,'' he answered in a dangerously soft voice. ''You're over twenty-one. Not all men would have behaved in as fatherly a way as the cabdriver did who brought you here. Some man might take your costume and the fact that you're alone in this part of town as a come-on.

''You're not exactly unattractive, even with that garish makeup. Anyone looking for a good time wouldn't have a clue that you're running away from a bad situation.''

At the accuracy of his observations, Kit felt the blood drain from her face. ''What makes you think I'm running away?''

''Not even a fool would venture outside in the dead of winter without a decent pair of shoes. Dance slippers can hardly be equated with the real thing. What puzzles me is why you're outfitted like that when you're not a dancer.''

She reached for the bedside table to brace herself and the money fell from her hand. This doctor saw too much!

''Would you care to explain that remark?'' She knew the white feathered costume was molded to her hips and rounded breasts as if made for her. What gave her away?

''You're slender as the result of diet, not exercise. Your body is smooth, but your muscles are soft. Your delicate feet have never seen the inside of a toe shoe. Your air of a graceful swan does not disguise a body whose muscles should have been built to whipcord strength."

Kit groaned in defeat.

"You're an enigma for the moment. You keep your nails well manicured, your hair smells sweet and has a healthy gloss. Your teeth are remarkably white and perfect—all of which tells its own story."

Her head came up in alarm. "I don't think you're a doctor at all!"

His lips quirked. "In my profession I'm called many things. Your command of the English language tells me even more about you." His half smile was wicked, and it was difficult to remain indignant. "The fact that you'd like to tell me I'm a bastard, and can't, reveals more than you can imagine. Now, I suggest you go into the adjoining bathroom and take off that makeup before I have to treat you for a rash. Most people's skin won't be used to the irritants of theatrical greasepaint."

She put her hands to her cheeks. His clairvoyance astounded her. Already the itching sensation had become unbearable. She was one of those people who couldn't tolerate Pan-Cake makeup.

His hands went to his back pockets, drawing her attention to his hard-muscled thighs. "I won't be too long. Don't get any ideas about running away. The doors can't be opened without the remote and the downstairs windows have bars." He plucked the bill from the floor. "I think I'll take you up on your humble offering." After pocketing it, he said,

"In the morning, we'll see about getting you a *real* pair of shoes, among other things."

Taking her silence as capitulation, he left the examining room. The moment he disappeared, Kit went into the bathroom to take a look at herself. The mirror revealed a face out of a tragicomedy. No makeup above her eyes—a ghoulish caricature of a swan below.

She removed as much of the greasepaint as she could with toilet paper, then found the lotion he'd mentioned and rubbed it into her skin. Though he'd disconcerted her with his uncanny powers of observation, Kit knew a deep gratitude for his help. He'd taken her in after hours, without any thought of payment.

After three applications, all traces of the makeup were gone. Blotchy patches on her freshly scrubbed face and an ugly red lump with a patch that would eventually discolor marred her usual creamy complexion.

She heard a knock on the bathroom door. When she opened it, some clothes were thrust into her arms. "These won't fit, but they're the best I can do on such short notice." She felt his eyes rest on her features, but they were veiled so she couldn't tell what he was thinking. "The driver was right. You shouldn't be out on your own after dark."

Kit avoided his level gaze. "I had my reasons," she said in a low voice, but couldn't disguise the tremor. If only he knew the truth... A shiver of fear uncurled in the pit of her stomach.

"I'd like to hear them."

She sensed the sincerity behind his words before he walked away. Her eyes darted to the pajamas and robe. He couldn't really keep her here if she wanted to leave. Faced with the alternative of taking another taxi to a shelter, where a man stalking her might think to look, the doctor's offer of hospitality sounded more and more attractive. She really couldn't be in better hands, even if he was a stranger.

Within minutes, she'd put on the striped flannel pajamas and dark brown velour robe, all of which were meant to be worn by a man of Dr. Banning's dimensions. Still, they felt warm and comfortable.

She cinched the belt tightly around her waist to keep the bottoms from falling off and rolled up the legs so she could walk without tripping. This way, she felt a little better prepared to face this man whose powers of deduction fitted her image of a truly professional doctor.

Sighing with weariness and a headache that throbbed with each heartbeat, she carried the tights and costume out of the bathroom.

"Put those things on the chair and come with me," he called to her from the hallway.

She did his bidding and followed him through a door at the end of the corridor that connected with the rear of the house. Looking at him, she would have thought he lived his life in the outdoors. His solid, masculine strength suggested physical activity and stamina, destroying any concept she might have harbored that the internists of her acquaintance were too cerebral and married to their work.

Kit felt a strange unreality about being in this man's clinic, wearing his clothes and entering his living quarters, which lacked the usual furnishings and pictures.

"I closed on this place six weeks ago," he said, reading her mind again. "It's taken me the better part of a month to equip the front offices so I could open for business. It will be a while before I get around to decorating the place." He flashed her a charming, lopsided smile, which she tentatively returned.

The kitchen was large and adequate, but the whole room could use some remodeling. Right now, of course, it represented a haven. Kit wanted to stay there forever and pretend that the world didn't spawn lunatics who terrorized their helpless victims until they'd lost their minds, or their lives, or both.

"I don't know about you," he murmured as a shadow crossed over her face, "but I'm ravenous." He held out one of two folding chairs placed around a card table that had seen better days. "While you were removing your makeup, I made us something to eat."

Kit stirred at the sound of his voice and sat down. At his urging, she helped herself to a chicken sandwich and some potato chips. Everything tasted delicious, and to her surprise, she found that she was hungry.

Judging by the way the food disappeared, the doctor hadn't eaten for some time, either. How strange that only an hour ago she'd been at the ballet and had known nothing of this man's existence. Yet now, she ate at his table, dressed in his clothes and accepted his hospitality.

Maybe she'd lost touch with reality, and striking her head had hastened the process.

"Relax," he admonished. "Enjoy your meal," he added over the rim of his coffee mug. "There's plenty more if you want a second helping."

Kit looked across at him, touched by his kindness. "Thank you. For everything." Her lip quivered.

She felt his puzzled gaze wander over her, as if she were some kind of riddle for which he must find a solution. Faint lines of weariness etched beneath his eyes and around his mouth tugged at her. He'd answered the taxi driver's summons after hours. Because of her, he'd lost precious time and, possibly, sleep.

"Since you admit you owe me something, why not start by telling me your name?" he said with amazing perception, offering her coffee, which she refused.

"It's Linda," she lied.

"You don't look like a Linda," he inserted softly, giving her a chance to tell him the truth, but she couldn't. "The cabdriver said you were screaming as you ran up to the car. Be honest. You were running from something or someone when you fell on the ice tonight."

Kit took a deep breath and tried to think. After tomorrow morning, she'd never see the doctor again and didn't dare leave any clues as to her real identity.

He waited, then rubbed his bottom lip with the pad of his thumb. "It might help to talk about it. Oftentimes, what we fear most is fear itself. I know it's a cliché, but that's why it was coined in the first place, because there's so much truth in it."

Kit massaged her temple as if merely touching it would make her headache disappear. "Look, Dr. Banning," she blurted, "it's not what you think, and I can't bear to talk about it." Her voice shook.

He leaned forward. "If you're trying to protect your husband or your boyfriend, remember that anything you divulge to me is confidential."

She shook her head. "I'm not married and this has absolutely nothing to do with a boyfriend."

His brows furrowed into an uncompromising line. "You haven't been physically abused. I've witnessed that for myself. But other damage has been done."

"Yes."

"You're frightened."

After a long silence, she said, "I'm terrified."

"I believe you. Otherwise you wouldn't have done anything quite so desperate, but why the homeless shelter? That's where the taxi driver said he picked you up. Did you honestly have no place else to go? No one to whom you might have turned for help?"

"No." She lifted a tormented face to him. "No place is safe. That's what's so horrifying."

He stared hard at her. "You're tired. If you don't get to bed soon, you might slip off that chair," he drawled. "You'll be safe and comfortable in the examining room. I'll check on you during the night in case you develop complications. In the morning, everything will look better."

Thankful that the interrogation was over, Kit nodded. She was tired—desperately so.

"You'll find new toothbrushes in the medicine cabinet. I bought them in the event that my nephew and niece come and spend the night with me."

Kit rose from the table oddly reassured by his mention of family. A man in his mid- to late thirties would in all probability have a wife and children. Yet something in his words led her to believe he didn't.

"Good night, Dr. Banning. Thank you again." She hoped she wouldn't disgrace herself by stumbling over his pajama legs as she made her exit.

"I'll be there shortly to tuck you in," he said, adding the first note of levity to their conversation, but Kit couldn't appreciate it.

"Y-you won't tell anyone I'm here, will you?"

His steady gaze locked with hers. "Whom would I tell?"

"The police, maybe?"

"Why? Have you killed someone?" he asked in the same calm voice he would use with a child.

"No. Actually, I—I'm afraid someone is going to kill me."

He considered her response, then said, "Nothing will bother you here. You're safe." Miraculously, he left it alone.

Under ordinary circumstances, Kit might have had trouble going to sleep in such unfamiliar clinical surroundings, but the doctor engendered such feelings of trust and security, she was out almost before her head touched the pillow.

When he came into the room to cover her with an extra blanket, she was scarcely aware of his presence, or of his wishing her sweet dreams.

The next morning, the tantalizing aroma of hot coffee and bacon wafted past Kit's nostrils, arousing her from a deep sleep. She stirred.

"So, you're awake at last." A vibrant male voice caused Kit to peer out from under the covers.

She had trouble focusing. It was the first night in weeks that she hadn't been plagued by nightmares and disorienting dreams. The headache had diminished and the goose egg on her forehead didn't seem as big.

"In case you don't remember, you're in my clinic."

Kit came fully awake and experienced a fresh stab of guilt, not only because he made her feel safe and pampered, and she wanted to hold on to the moment, but because he was still waiting on her and she couldn't repay him yet.

"W-what time is it?" she asked, burrowing into the mattress to keep her head covered so Dr. Banning couldn't get a good look.

"Late enough that I debated whether to bring you breakfast or lunch."

A soft gasp escaped. Like a penitent child, she reluctantly sat up and propped her back against the wall. Embarrassed, she smoothed her hair into some kind of order. When she noticed that he was watching her, she blushed, which was absurd. He was a doctor, for heaven's sake.

"You don't look at all like the wounded swan I unfolded from that satin cape last night, *Linda*." She knew he'd underlined the word to make her feel uncomfortable. "Why don't you eat this while it's still hot?" He put the tray on her lap.

The bacon and scrambled eggs looked delicious. So did the toast. "Thank you, Dr. Banning." Since he stood there acting like he had no intention of going away, she had little choice but to start eating. She found she was hungry and in a few minutes she'd devoured everything on the plate and had drunk her orange juice.

With a nod of satisfaction, he took away the tray and returned shortly with some packages, which he put on the end of the bed. His half smile filled her with unaccustomed warmth, making her heart turn over. "I've been out shopping and had to guess about sizes."

Her attention had been so taken with his tall, masculine frame dressed in a black turtleneck and jeans, it took her a second to register what he'd said. "You bought clothes for me?" Her voice came out more like a squeak. *He was an incredible man.*

"I rather liked the look of you in that fetching costume, but I presume you'll be more comfortable in something that keeps you warm."

"Thank you," she whispered. A slow smile lit up her countenance, revealing a natural, womanly beauty that her fear had masked last night.

He took her wrist and checked the pulse, then examined her forehead. "The swelling has gone down. Do you want something for pain?"

"No." Kit shook her head. "I dislike relying on pills unless I have to take them. I'm really feeling much better, thanks to you."

"You look refreshed. A good night's sleep often cures what medicine can't. When I checked on you last night, you were sleeping peacefully. I can tell the rest has been beneficial."

"I feel like a new person," Kit said, drawing her knees to her chest beneath the covers. "And since you've been kind enough to buy me some clothes, I'll get dressed and be on my way. When I can, I'll pay you back."

All she needed was something like a scarf to hide her hair until she could buy a wig. If he could help her with that, then she wouldn't ask for another favor.

To her surprise, his face suddenly sobered and he removed the morning newspaper from one of the sacks. Kit's feeling of well-being evaporated when he dropped it across her knees. "Why don't you get dressed and then come back to the kitchen?" On that note, he strode out of the room.

Kit looked down and fastened her attention on one of the headlines.

Disappearance Of Stragi-Corp Employee Baffles Police.

Kit stifled a cry and continued to read.

Twenty-five-year-old Kathryn Mitchell, newest chemical engineer to join the Stragi-Corp firm, was last seen attending a performance of *Swan Lake* last night at the Capitol Theater.

According to Ross Hunter, Ms. Mitchell's brother-in-law, he and his wife left her at intermission to chat with friends. When they returned, she was missing.

Aghast that her disappearance was already public knowledge, she studied the pictures.

A photographer had caught Laura and Ross in front of the theater. The up-and-coming hopeful for the governorship always drew a lot of press. But in this photo, his conventionally handsome features were marred by a distraught expression that could or could not be considered genuine.

At this point, Kit was so paranoid she felt unbalanced and quickly looked at the shot of herself. Someone had given the press a picture she'd had taken for her university placement file while she'd been job hunting. It was more professional than glamorous.

She scanned the rest of the write-up. "Police Suspect Foul Play And Have Called In FBI" read a smaller headline. The final paragraph mentioned

that anyone knowing anything of her whereabouts
was to contact the police immediately.

When there wasn't anything more to read, she
threw down the paper, her first thought being that
she'd put Dr. Banning in an untenable position.
According to the article, any parties knowingly
withholding information faced serious consequences, even possible prosecution.

Taking a deep breath, she pushed the covers aside
and got out of bed. The sooner she disappeared
from Dr. Banning's clinic, the better.

She reached for the first sack, which contained
an entire wardrobe. Underwear, a cream-colored,
cotton-knit pullover, several T-shirts, a couple pairs
of jeans, sneakers, stockings, a parka and even a
handbag, lipstick and comb.

Hot tears spilled down her cheeks. His big heart
would prove to be a drain on his pocketbook even
if he had a lucrative practice. Kit certainly couldn't
fault his taste.

She took a quick shower, washed her hair and
dressed in the new clothes, marveling that he had
such an accurate eye for size and color. She combed
her black hair into its usual casual style. Even wet,
the natural curl tended to make it a bit unruly. Her
hand shook as she applied the pink frosted lipstick
he'd picked out.

Dr. Banning understood human nature very well,
she mused. Outfitting her like this gave her back
some dignity. He'd sensed all these things, just as
he'd sensed that she hadn't begun to explain her
bizarre behavior.

Other than the bandage that would have to stay in place for another day, Kit finally felt ready to thank him one last time for all he'd done before she faced the unknown.

She made the bed, laid his pajamas and robe across the end, then hurried to the kitchen. He turned when he saw her appear in the doorway. His assessing blue eyes swept over her without revealing his thoughts.

"That's quite a transformation, Ms. Mitchell."

CHAPTER TWO

KIT'S rounded chin lifted a trifle. "I owe it all to you." Her husky voice held a slight tremor. "The clothes are wonderful. A perfect fit. I promise to repay you when I can. Under the circumstances, I think it's best if I leave now, before you get any more involved."

He didn't say anything and she grew more nervous. "After reading the paper, I realize that it's only a matter of time before the taxi driver tells the police what happened last night. If I'm gone, you'll be able to answer their questions without any problem."

His continued silence disconcerted her. "I—I'm sorry to have mixed you up in this, Dr. Banning. I've placed you in a horrible position. Sometimes I wish I were dead," she whispered.

"Don't ever say that! It's not an answer," he snapped, barely controlling his anger. "While I do a little cooking for the dinner we're going to have later, I suggest you start paying me back by explaining whatever it is that has been eating you alive."

"But the longer I stay here—"

"In case you haven't noticed," he cut in, "we had more snow last night. It's possible the taxi driver hasn't heard the news and is busy picking up fares who can't drive today. I doubt very much he'll connect the picture of the studious-looking engineer wearing glasses and a blazer with the haunted swan he picked up last night. Your disguise was too perfect. Even I would have been completely fooled if I hadn't examined you."

"Was it really that good?"

His eyes kindled with a strange light. "There's no way he could look at you right now and think you are either of those women.

"If he's exceptionally perceptive, it might dawn on him in a month or two and he might come forward with what he knows. But I'm convinced that for now I'm the only human being in the Mountain West who knows where you are. And since you're our state's number one priority, I think that entitles me to some answers."

Kit sank into one of the chairs and watched him put a roast in the oven. He flicked her a piercing glance as he shut the door.

"Last night, I treated a woman who seemed terrified of her own shadow. Why don't we start there?"

"A-all right." She took a shuddering breath. "About two months ago, I entered my office and found a note on my desk. It was a simple type-written message and it said, 'I'm watching you, Kit Mitchell, and one day I'm going to get you.' She couldn't control the tremor in her voice.

"You go by Kit?"

"Only to my closest friends."

"Go on."

"At first, I presumed it was a joke. There aren't very many women who work at Stragi-Corp and the ones who do are secretaries, not engineers. Since the men who work on the same projects with me like to tease me a lot, I thought nothing of it and tossed the note in the wastebasket. Two days later, I found the same kind of note stuck inside the day planner on my desk.

"At that point, I asked people if they knew anything about it, if they'd seen anything, but the answer was no. Jeremy told me it was probably a jealous colleague who'd been passed over. To forget it. I tried doing just that, but then something worse happened."

"Who's Jeremy?"

"The CEO." Too agitated to remain seated, Kit got to her feet. "I live alone in a condo on the Avenues with good security. When I found another note stuck in the corner of my dresser mirror, you can imagine how it alarmed me. Particularly because another line had been added to the threat. It said that my days were numbered."

"I hope you called the police."

"Actually, I called my sister, Laura. She and Ross Hunter, her husband, came right over. When I explained what happened, Ross called the police."

Dr. Banning stood with his back to the counter, a raw potato in his hand. "What did they say?"

"The police felt it had to be a prank carried out by someone who knew me well. They suggested that my boss was probably right, that it was a disgruntled employee. They put a man on the case.

"After that, I felt a little better because the police had started an investigation. But my fear escalated when a week later I found another note stuck in the pocket of my lab coat at work. And two weeks after that I found an identical note in my suit jacket, which had been hanging in my condo closet.

"The investigating officer couldn't account for it and more men were called in. When I told Laura, she and Ross insisted that I move in with them for a while. Ross arranged for police protection. So I closed up my condo and went to stay with them, but I hated intruding on their marriage. Still, I was terribly grateful because they're the only family I have left."

"Did you receive more notes when you moved in with your sister?"

"Yes. One came in the mail."

"The same message?"

"Always the same. Three days later, another one turned up in the newspaper delivered to their front door." She shook her head. "When that happened, I told Jeremy that I was going to take a leave of absence from work. If he felt he had to let me go, it was all right.

"He told me not to worry about it, that my job was secure. He could see what this was doing to me, how it affected my work. It didn't matter that I had police protection because the notes kept showing up in spite of everything."

"What did the crime lab uncover?"

She shrugged. "Absolutely nothing. The police are stymied and they can't afford to give me round-the-clock protection anymore. So I've been staying at my sister's and have stopped going out for any reason."

"And the notes keep coming."

"Yes." Her lower lip trembled. "Another one turned up taped to the back door. I'm afraid I went to pieces. If Laura and Ross hadn't been in the house when it happened, I don't know what I would have done.

"Ross got angry and demanded more police protection. The problem is, my sister has been a bit high-strung since losing the baby she was carrying. She's found it difficult to conceive. This situation has put her on the verge of a nervous breakdown, and Ross is beside himself."

"Didn't the police bring in guard dogs?"

"Yes. But as soon as they did that, the notes stopped coming. For three weeks, there weren't any. Nothing. The police said that the sick person responsible had probably grown bored and given it up. I'd hoped so, too, until last night...."

He finished peeling the potatoes, then sat down opposite her. "What happened?"

"Ross felt it wasn't healthy for me to stay indoors all the time—that I needed to get out. He had tickets for the ballet and insisted that we go. I know he was trying desperately hard to cheer me and Laura up—I think to prove to us that he had quit worrying. He even called off the dogs. His optimism gave me the courage, and since I adore the ballet, I wanted to believe that the nightmare had ended—that I could start living again."

Kit paced the floor, wrapping her arms around her waist. "At intermission, they left to go talk to friends. While I thumbed through the program, I found another note," she continued shakily. "But this one was different. It said, 'Tonight's the night, Kit Mitchell.'" She lifted her head and looked straight at Dr. Banning. "I've never been so terrified in my life. The person stalking me was in the audience and was watching me. I fell apart."

"I can imagine," he murmured sympathetically.

"I'm sorry, Dr. Banning, but I don't think you can. I don't think anyone can who hasn't been through this sort of thing. Something snapped inside of me and I ran for Laura and Ross. But I couldn't find them. Then I saw this man in the lobby and I thought he looked strangely at me and I panicked."

"There'd have to be a security guard on duty. Why didn't you speak to him?"

"What could he have done when the police department hasn't been able to figure out anything?"

"Quite a lot, but putting that aside, what did you do next?"

"I made the decision to disappear."

"You're very resourceful to have found your way backstage and disguised yourself in that costume."

"I was desperate."

"How did you get rid of your things?"

"I flushed the contents of my wallet down the toilet and hid my clothes and purse in the bottom of a basket of ballet slippers. I had about forty-five dollars on me, which I kept. Then I ran out the fire-escape door and down the alley.

"The same man I'd seen in the lobby was standing at the end, just as if he'd been waiting for me. That's when I screamed and started running for the taxi. If I hadn't fallen and hit my head, I'd have spent a night at the Salvation Army and would be on my way to someplace else today."

He pursed his lips. "Maybe. Maybe not. Nevertheless, the police have most likely found everything out by now even if it didn't come out in the newspaper. Naturally, your disappearance has been linked to the other problem. A mystery within a mystery."

She came to a standstill. "I've told you the truth. All I want is to lose myself and begin a new life someplace else." Swallowing hard, she said, "If you could buy me a wig, it's all I'd need to get away from here unrecognized. I'll pay you back, I swear it."

"What are your plans?"

She straightened. "To get as far away from here as possible."

"I mean specific plans."

"I thought I'd buy a bus ticket and ride as far into Nevada as possible. Then I'd look for a job cleaning a motel. You don't always have to have references for work like that."

Lines darkened his face. "I find your fear perfectly reasonable, but what you're proposing will only buy you momentary respite from your problem. It won't solve the fact that someone with a disorder means you harm and is still running around loose.

"If this person is never apprehended, you could conceivably spend the rest of your life living with an impossible burden of fear, forfeiting your right to live your life the way destiny intended. Is that what you want?"

"Of course it's not what I want," she asserted, unable to fight her tears. "But I'm so frightened that I can't think or function normally anymore. I know I sound psychotic."

"Not at all. You're suffering from a phobic reaction for perfectly legitimate reasons."

"I hate it. My problem has disrupted the entire family. I've hurt my career and made trouble for the project at work. Any social life I had is nonexistent because at this point I don't trust a living soul except Laura."

He cocked his head. "You don't trust your brother-in-law?"

There was a slight pause. "Yes. Yes, of course I do," she blurted, her gray-green eyes flashing. "But the police said this person had to be someone close to me, and I have to assume that Ross would be included on any list made up by the police. Don't you see? I have to get away before I lose my sanity and destroy everyone else's around me!"

"And you don't think that running away has upset your sister?"

Kit put a shaky hand to her throat. "I plan to call her and let her know I'm all right as soon as I get to Nevada."

"Which could take some time," he muttered beneath his breath. "For someone you love and trust so implicitly, I find it rather odd that you're not on the phone right now to reassure her."

She couldn't meet his gaze. "If you must know, I accidentally overheard Laura and Ross talking one night. Laura was distraught and asked Ross if he thought I had made up the whole thing to get attention because I was missing my father," she confessed reluctantly. It still hurt to think her own sister could have entertained the idea.

"So you're punishing your sister for not believing in you," he concluded. "Yet you readily admit your sister has been under a strain since she miscarried."

"You make me sound like a monster!"

"I'm merely repeating back what you're telling me," he said on an even note.

She pondered his observations for a long moment. "Maybe I do want to hurt Laura, but I didn't realize it until now."

"You wouldn't be human if you didn't want to strike out at the one person who loves you unconditionally."

"But does she?"

"Doesn't she?" he returned forcefully. "Mightn't you have asked the same question about her if your roles had been reversed? You admit the police haven't come up with any clues."

"No, I wouldn't have, because I know Laura, and she isn't capable of manufacturing a lie like that."

He pushed himself up from the chair and walked toward her. "Let me tell you something, Kit—if I may call you that?" he asked softly.

She nodded.

"A human being is capable of anything, given the right set of circumstances."

She stiffened. "Are you saying you think I made the whole thing up?"

"Did you?"

Her features froze. "No."

"I believe you."

She let out a breath she didn't know she'd been holding.

"How badly would you like to see this deranged person caught?"

"I'd do anything if I thought it was possible."

"Do you believe that anything is possible?"

Her heart began to pound harder. "Before this happened, I would have said yes."

"Would you be willing to put yourself in my hands until the culprit is apprehended?"

"Look, Dr. Banning. I've intruded in your life too long already. I'm not quite sure what you're getting at, but I couldn't possibly impose anymore."

"You wouldn't be imposing if you accepted a position as my receptionist for a temporary period."

"What?"

"Hiring someone to answer the phone and make appointments is the next order of business on my agenda. As I explained earlier, I'm still in the process of opening my clinic. You could help me get my files and paperwork organized."

Kit was taken aback. "But why would you do this for me? I don't understand."

"Your case is not only unique, it's bizarre. Naturally, I'd like to see you embrace life again for your own sake. I also admit that I'm curious about this person who's terrorizing you.

"In medical practice, we may have occasion to work with the law when a criminal element enters the picture. I have a good friend, now retired from a top position in the Denver police department, who lives in Summit County and takes the odd case with an unusual twist, like yours. I'd like your permission to contact him and explain the situation."

"But he won't be able to help."

"Trust me, Kit. This man is good. If I were in your shoes, he's the one I'd want on my team. He'll work out the fee after the case is closed.

"If he took you on as a client, you'd be his sole priority. Of necessity, you'd have to be accessible to him on his terms. If you worked for me, we could make your daily schedule flexible to accommodate his."

Slowly, Kit wandered over to the sink and looked out the window. Nothing moved outside. They were cocooned in a white world. "I don't know what to think. The idea of having to go through any more of this appalls me."

He came up behind her. "You don't have to make a decision right now. Merely think about it. You're welcome to remain under my roof until you're ready to go on, one way or the other."

She glanced over her shoulder at him, drawing strength from his wise counsel. She envied him his ability to remain unshakable. "You must think me the most ungrateful, selfish woman on earth."

The light of compassion entered his eyes. "You've been the victim of a set of circumstances totally beyond your control. The fact that you attended the ballet last night tells a great deal about the courage and determination inside Kit Mitchell.

"But you're up against something that is going to require outside help if you want to be free. I'm prepared to offer that help in exchange for your assistance. Gratitude doesn't enter into it."

"You're a good man, Dr. Banning. Your patients must be legion."

His lips twitched. "Your decision will tell me just how effective I am as a doctor." Kit averted her eyes. "Whatever the outcome, there's still the problem of a temporary disguise for you. Contrary to popular belief, most men still prefer brunettes, but if you'll trust me, I'll try to pick out a wig in a shade of blond that will throw anyone off the scent."

A smile came and went on her lips and she chanced another glance at him. "I look ghastly as a blonde so that should be a good choice—especially if it's long hair."

His gaze played over her features and she felt a funny little skip of her heartbeat. "Not ghastly. Wild, maybe exotic, but not ghastly."

He stood close enough for her to feel the warmth of his body and smell the faint aroma of some wonderful after-shave with a woody flavor. She noticed his chin was aggressively firm, but displayed a slight hint of a cleft.

Since graduation, she'd dated a couple of men from work. Nothing serious. Dinner and a movie. They were very nice and into their jobs the way she was. None of them compared to Dr. Banning. In fact, she'd never met anyone like him. For want of a better word, he seemed complete. A total man. One in whom she had implicit trust.

She took a deep breath. "While you're out, you'd better buy me a uniform of some kind. If I'm going to be your receptionist, I need to look the part. And maybe a pair of glasses without a correction— to play down my wild, untamed image."

A faint, secretive smile broke the corner of his mouth, frightening her in a strange new way because, with those few words, she'd committed herself to his plan.

His strong, steady hand reached out and cupped her chin. "You're a fighter, Kit, and that means everything," he said with intense feeling, yet sounding very far away. Then his hand dropped. "I'm going out now. If I have trouble finding what I'm looking for, how would you feel about being a redhead?"

"Red hair might make me look a little too flashy, hardly the image you're trying to establish at your clinic."

"Oh, I don't know," he teased with disarming frankness. "For your information, I've turned over my calls to an answering service and I want to keep it that way for the rest of the day, so don't be tempted to pick up the phone. If you want to watch television, there's a small set in my bedroom, along with a few books and magazines. Make yourself at home.

"If you get hungry, the refrigerator and cupboards are fairly well stocked. And if you're really ambitious," he emphasized, "you could place the potatoes around the roast in another half hour."

Kit lifted her well-shaped nose in the air. "So all along it's a cook you've been after. I hate to disappoint you, but it's been years since I fixed a meal from scratch."

His low chuckle floated back at her as he left the kitchen in a few long strides. It was a happy sound.

Strangely enough, now that she'd made the decision to stay and accept his help, she felt herself relax as she hadn't done in ages.

Meeting him constituted some sort of miracle. Nothing about her situation had changed, but she suddenly felt alive again and free from paralyzing fear.

On a new burst of energy, she acquainted herself with his kitchen and decided to drum up a dessert for their dinner. Perhaps she'd surprise him with her chocolate mint brownies, if she could find all the ingredients. They had been her father's favorite food, the only recipe she'd committed to memory.

To her surprise, she was able to locate nearly everything except the mint flavoring and the chocolate. In their place, she substituted vanilla and cocoa, which worked equally well, then spooned the dough into a baking pan. When the roast and potatoes were done, she'd bake the brownies.

Now that she had time on her hands, she decided to take a tour of his house. It had a certain graciousness because of the high ceilings and ornate wood moldings. Furnished properly, it could be very attractive.

Except for the kitchen, all the other rooms on the main floor had been converted to a clinic. She assumed the laundry room was in the basement. The upper floor contained three bedrooms and two bathrooms. One of the bedrooms stood empty. Another bedroom with a window seat appeared partly furnished with two twin beds, nothing else.

Dr. Banning's bedroom contained an unmade king-size bed. An open suitcase sat on the only chair in the room and there were still some clothes in it. Feeling as if she was trespassing, she retraced her steps. But as she started out the door, her eye caught sight of a framed photograph on the dresser.

She recognized one of the boys on horseback as Dr. Banning. The older boy had to be a brother because there was an unmistakable resemblance. They were probably around sixteen and eighteen, youthfully handsome and vital, emerging into men.

Kit stared at the picture for a few minutes before going downstairs, anxious to familiarize herself with the receptionist's office. It was the first room to the right of the front door with the doctor's study directly behind it.

Like the rest of the main floor, it was carpeted in a forest green broadloom. The off-white walls

and dark walnut stain on the moldings achieved a
quiet elegance that reassured rather than intimidated. Rich or poor needing his services would feel
comfortable here.

A secretarial unit had been installed along with
a file cabinet, computer and keyboard, telephone
intercom. But boxes stacked against the back wall
indicated that nothing had been put away in drawers
and cupboards. Several hours of sorting would be
required to get everything in order.

Kit didn't mind office work. In her teens, she'd
often helped her dad out in the summer when one
of his secretaries at the law firm went on vacation.
She determined to be the best receptionist possible
in exchange for the doctor's help.

For want of anything else to do, she plunged into
the job of unpacking supplies sent out from a local
office outfitter and began arranging drawers and
shelves according to her own system.

Discovering a clock radio, she plugged it in and
turned on a classical music station that happened
to be broadcasting a taped performance from the
Met. She loved classical and had always done her
studies to it.

"You didn't have to build Rome in a day."

At the sound of Dr. Banning's low voice she
wheeled around and quickly turned off the radio,
embarrassed to be caught humming.

"I hope you don't mind that I've put things
away."

He shed his sheepskin jacket, never taking his
eyes off her. "For the time being, reception is your

department. Why would I mind?'' He tossed his coat with careless grace over the back of a chair. ''How's our dinner coming along?''

''The dinner!''

Kit dashed out of the room and into the kitchen to check on it. He made an appearance as she put the brownies in the oven.

''I just phoned Dart Thueson, the private investigator I told you about. His wife took the message and said he'd call me this evening, so I've told the service to ring through. As a word of caution, before you call your sister to let her know you're all right, Dart will want to hear the facts so he can advise you on exactly what to say to her.''

The mention of Laura took the joy out of the moment. Kit's eyes clouded in distress. For a little while, she'd managed to separate herself from fear. *And all because of the pleasure in being in Dr. Banning's fascinating company.*

Without stopping to consider the consequences, she'd placed her life, her sanity, in the hands of a man she hardly knew. Maybe she'd finally gone over the edge....

CHAPTER THREE

"I THINK your dinner is ready," she informed him after he'd washed his hands in the kitchen sink.

"That's good. I've been salivating ever since I entered the house."

He reached in the cupboard for a bottle of red wine, insisting a little alcohol would relax her. Then they sat down for their meal, which—if Kit's mother had been alive—she would have praised.

After a few bites, she exclaimed, "This food is incredibly delicious. If there's ever a revolution and doctors go out of style—"

"Heaven forbid," he interjected with mock severity.

She chuckled. "As I was saying, you could be a chef. The rich will always be able to pay for a fabulous meal somehow."

His level gaze played over her features. "If that were the case, I'd probably go back to full-time ranching."

Her instincts had been right. He was a man who loved the out-of-doors. It explained the family photograph propped on his dresser.

"What about you?" he asked before she could formulate her next question. For some strange reason, she had this growing desire to know more about him.

"What do you mean?"

"When chemical engineers are no longer in demand, how will you exist?"

"I'm not worried," she said with a teasing smile. "My statics professor told me that if the day ever came when we weren't needed, it would mean that it was the end of the world, so it wouldn't matter. That's why I decided to go into my profession."

Dr. Banning broke into full-bodied laughter.

Kit sipped her wine slowly, trying not to stare at his white smile, the way his amazing blue eyes lit up, making him the most attractive man she'd ever met in her life.

Enjoying a meal with him could become addicting. By the time they were ready for dessert, she'd discovered that he could converse brilliantly on any subject and had managed to elicit her laughter several times relating anecdotes connected with his practice.

Wiping the corner of her mouth with a paper napkin, she said, "Tell me about your schedule, Dr. Banning. What it is exactly that I'm to do? I realize that the people who come to you may have both physical and emotional problems. I don't want to add to their distress by saying the wrong thing."

Dr. Banning leaned forward, elbows on the table. "They're human beings, just like you and me. Be your normal self. As for a schedule, I'm still undecided how best to divide my time between here and the clinic in Heber."

"You practice in Heber?" The small farming community in the Wasatch Mountains about forty

miles southeast of Salt Lake was one of her favorite places.

"Yes. My practice is spread throughout that part
of the county. I think we'll have to plan for things
a week at a time. There are too many unknowns at
the moment to predict beyond that."

Her brow furrowed. "Because of me."

"Wrong, Ms. Mitchell." He drained his wine-
glass. "Hiring you has solved a big problem for
me," he stated cryptically.

Something significant was going on inside him.
She had the distinct feeling that his mind had focused somwhere else, that his thoughts were dark,
possibly forbidding.

"May I ask why you're commuting between here
and the mountains?"

"My practice has grown to the point where the
greater portion of my patients lives in Salt Lake.
Until nine months ago, when my brother was killed
after being thrown from a horse, we ran a clinic
together. His specialty was psychiatry. We had the
perfect arrangement and oftentimes collaborated
on criminal cases that had to be handled by the
courts in Salt Lake."

"Is that how you met Mr. Thueson?" she
interjected.

"Exactly. Since my brother's death, I've gravi-
tated toward the idea of practicing exclusively in
Salt Lake for the obvious reasons of time and prac-
ticality. Relocating, however, entails phasing out
slowly and—" he paused "—I have ties to Heber
that will always draw me back."

"Like a wife and children?" She asked the question that had been torturing her until she could hardly think about anything else.

"My niece and nephew," he replied in a low, mocking voice. "Now, to get down to specifics ..." He changed the subject abruptly, closing the door on anything more personal. "I'll keep office hours next week from nine to four. The appointment book is in my office. Tomorrow being Sunday, you'll have ample time to look it over and see what lies ahead. One of your duties will be to call patients the day before they're due to come in, to remind them, to verify the time, and so on."

"When new patients call in for an appointment, how do I handle them?"

"I'll take those calls for the time being. It all depends on their location and urgency. When I have patients in the hospital, I make my rounds before nine. Any more questions?"

"Several, actually." She darted him an anxious glance. "When do you go back to Heber?"

"Next weekend, and I'll remain there for the next ten days."

"I see." For an inexplicable reason she felt bereft at the idea of his going away.

He chuckled softly. "I doubt it. You'll be coming with me, of course. Dart retired to Heber and lives two miles from the ranch. You'll be spending quite a little time with him while he compiles a history on you. He's nothing if not thorough. It pays dividends in the end."

Kit felt guilty at the relief spreading through her, already aware that she was becoming too dependent on him. Maybe all his patients felt the same way. He radiated confidence and authority. Twenty-four hours in his company had given her a secure, almost carefree feeling, which was ridiculous considering she still didn't know the identity of the person terrorizing her.

The sound of the phone ringing had Dr. Banning on his feet. "I'll take it in my office. Don't put the brownies away. I'll be back for more because they're sinfully rich, just the way I like my dessert."

Kit got up to do the dishes, needing to channel her energies with something physical. Dr. Banning spent quite a long time on the phone, causing her to wonder if Mr. Thueson needed persuading.

"Where are the rest of the brownies?" he asked the minute he entered the kitchen.

Kit whirled around, gesturing at the refrigerator. "Did you speak to Mr. Thueson?"

He reached for the pan and started eating while still standing up. "I did, and he agreed to take your case with unholy glee."

"Unholy?"

"Umm ... Dart eats, drinks and sleeps his particular line of work. The greater the challenge, the more excited he becomes. The mysterious disappearance of one Kit Mitchell has the Salt Lake Police Department in an uproar. I'm quoting him now. He gave out noises over the phone that sounded like the cat swallowing the canary.

"You'll like him, Kit. He wants to help. The particular psychopath who has made your life hell holds a certain fascination for him. He'll catch your stalker. Just give him time."

"You make it sound possible." Her voice shook with emotion.

"Believe it," he replied solemnly. "Two things..."

She flashed him a wary look.

"For reasons of his own, he doesn't want you contacting anyone until he meets with you next Saturday morning. He won't say anything to the police about my phone call to him.

"For starters, he's going to nose around, pick up information without anyone being aware. He knows you won't be happy about keeping your sister and brother-in-law in the dark, but the unusual circumstances in this case require unusual procedures.

"Of course, he can't stop you if you wish to call your sister, but he'd rather you didn't. Your original and clever disappearing act has provided him with an excellent opportunity to observe those concerned while everyone believes the worst. Once someone knows you're safe, it will change the complexion of the case. The choice, however, is *yours*," he emphasized.

Kit pondered his comments. A whole week of not knowing would tear Laura to pieces, but Kit could understand Mr. Thueson's reasoning.

"I want to do everything I can to catch the person responsible. The past twenty-four hours have proven to me that I can't go on living with this awful fear. It's not a life.''

He put the empty pan in the sink and turned to her. "Good for you. Now I suggest you get ready for bed. After that nasty fall last night, you need your rest. Plan to sleep in as long as you want. There'll be plenty of time tomorrow to rehearse your latest role. Have you decided on a name?''

"Linda Smith.''

"Still sticking to it, see," he drawled. "Well, it has an unoriginal, solid quality to it, which makes sense. Good night, Linda Smith. Tomorrow you can remove the bandage, and perhaps if you're up to it, you might transcribe notes off my tapes. I'm two weeks behind as it is.''

"Frankly I'll be glad to have something constructive to do.''

"Are you a workaholic?''

His question showed more than casual interest, and strangely enough, it bothered her. "Why do you ask?''

"Why do you take offense? Has someone suggested that your overtired brain has an equally overworked imagination?''

His ability to cut to the heart of the matter stunned her and a muffled sound escaped her throat. "Would you believe . . . everyone?''

"Loving your work is no sin, but it can arouse emotions of many kinds in those people who want a relationship with you. Think about it. Tomorrow evening, we'll explore Kit Mitchell's world as the newest whiz kid of the Stragi-Corp Company. *Your* perception, and the perception of those around you."

Kit wasn't sure she liked the sound of that.

"What's the matter?" he murmured. "Didn't you know that chemical engineers are put on a pedestal even higher than doctors? Most people less talented than you feel totally inadequate because you belong to an elite society that virtually makes our world run."

Her eyes grew huge because he understood so much about everything, about life!

"Tomorrow, we'll do a little role-playing. One of the most difficult things in the world is the ability to see ourselves as others see us. But when we can achieve this aim, the results are oftentimes a revelation."

He'd opened up an old wound and had given her a lot to think about. "Good night, Dr. Banning."

Kit felt his eyes on her retreating back as she left the kitchen and went to the front of the house, experiencing an unsettling sensation. During an ordinary conversation, he would suddenly become the doctor, possessing uncanny knowledge and perception.

He slipped in and out of his role as friend and confidant, becoming doctor and interrogator with an ease that threw her completely off balance.

Since nothing about their relationship was normal, she had no way of knowing what it would be like to meet him on a purely social basis, and then chastised herself for thinking about him in any other capacity than as a doctor.

When she finally climbed into bed, sleep didn't come for a long time. Lying on the cot in the sterile room, alone and in the dark, she felt as if she were caught up in a strange dream that had no basis in reality. But knowing that Dr. Banning had taken charge of her life brought a measure of peace that eventually allowed her to drift off.

She awakened late again the following morning and found several sacks by the side of her bed. Two of them contained a sweater and skirt, and a pale blue lab coat. In the other, she discovered a pair of glasses and a wig.

Excited by her find, Kit rushed to the bathroom, where she removed the bandage, then showered and dressed in the tan sweater and pleated tartan skirt. The wig came last.

A honey blond creation, it curved under her jawline in a pageboy style from a center part. The bangs almost touched her eyebrows. When she put on the tortoiseshell eyeglasses to complete the disguise, the transformation was miraculous.

She turned her head from side to side, delighted with her new image and the way the clothes fitted.

"Dr. Banning?" She raced to his office to thank him for everything. When she couldn't find him there, she hurried back to the kitchen, but he was nowhere in sight. Perhaps he'd gone to the hospital. Of course, there was always the possibility that he was still in bed, but she didn't dare go to his room to check.

While she waited for him to appear, she fixed some toast and juice. As the minutes ticked by, her elation faded and she decided she'd better get to work transcribing his tapes or go crazy.

No sooner had she settled down to the task than she heard the sound of the front door buzzer. It made her jump and immediately a dart of fear passed through her body. Anybody could be on the other side of that door. Maybe it was the police.

If Dr. Banning had been asleep, surely he'd have wakened by now. She sat perfectly still, praying that he would come down and answer the door, or that the person on the other side would go away.

The buzzer persisted, leading Kit to the conclusion that Dr. Banning had gone out while she'd been asleep. Slowly, she got up from the chair but her legs turned to jelly when whoever it was outside kept his finger on the buzzer. Someone wanted Dr. Banning desperately.

Perspiration beaded her forehead as she tiptoed to the foyer, listening for sounds.

"Uncle Jarod!" a boy called out at the top of his lungs. Now a rapping sound made by several pairs of hands against the door accompanied the buzzer.

Dr. Banning's family. Kit wanted to let them in but couldn't figure out how the lock worked.

"Jarod?" a woman's voice called out. "It's Lucy. Let us in." The knocking continued. "Chet? Look in the garage and see if his Land Rover's there."

"I already checked but there's no window," her son replied.

"He's probably asleep," the woman theorized. "Run around back and throw a snowball at his bedroom window. He must have worked late last night and is dead to the world.''

The mother sounded anxious and Kit worked harder than ever to discover the lock's secret. Just as she found the release and opened the door to his family, she heard glass shatter. Kit didn't know who looked more surprised.

While both women stood there in frozen silence, the daughter, who appeared to be about seven, ran past them, shouting back to her older brother, who had just come through the door, that he was in trouble for breaking Uncle Jarod's window.

"I'm sorry to have kept you standing there so long," Kit offered as she shut the door, hoping to placate Dr. Banning's sister-in-law, who walked toward the staircase, obviously out of sorts at having been forced to wait in the bitter cold.

She was smaller in stature than Kit's five-foot-seven frame and possessed a fragile blond beauty with becoming hollows in her pale cheeks. Dr. Banning had said he'd lost his brother less than a year ago, and if the two had been anything alike, then Kit felt great compassion for the woman's loss.

"I'm Lucy Banning, Jarod's sister-in-law," she announced, eyeing Kit condescendingly. "We decided to surprise him." She looked all around her, giving Kit time to study the woman's elegant chignon and caramel-colored mohair suit. She had to be in her early thirties, but retained a girl's youthful figure. "He's made quite a few improvements in the past week."

Finally, she gave Kit her full attention, fastening her light blue eyes on Kit's face and hair with a scrutiny that said she wasn't pleased.

"Did he get rid of Mrs. Baxter already?"

"I have no idea."

"When did you start cleaning for Jarod?"

"Yesterday." Kit played the innocent, sensing undercurrents here. "Actually, I've been hired to do typing and answer the phone."

"*You*?"

The woman's shock was so evident, Kit grew uneasy. This was a complication that she and the doctor hadn't discussed.

"What are you doing here on a Sunday?"

Grappling for the right response, she said, "Dr. Banning is anticipating a heavy schedule next week and kindly allowed me to come over and acquaint myself with the office. I'm still a litle nervous about working for a doctor and was starting to transcribe a tape when I heard the buzzer."

Once again, Kit felt Lucy Banning's gaze sweep over her with ill-disguised disdain. "What's your name?"

"Linda. Linda Smith."

"Well, Ms. Smith, don't let me keep you from your work. I'll go on upstairs and inspect the damage."

"*What damage*?"

Both heads turned at Dr. Banning's sudden appearance from the back of the house. A strange tension entered the room with him. His expression looked like thunder.

"Please don't be angry, Jarod. We thought you were sleeping. I told Chet to throw a snowball at your window. Forgive us," she begged and crossed the carpeted expanse to slip her arm through his and press a kiss to his cheek with the ease of longtime familiarity.

Dr. Banning appeared unmoved by her explanation. He transferred his cold gaze to Kit, who didn't know he could look that remote and unapproachable.

"Linda, please call A-1 Glass Company. They have a mobile unit that operates on a twenty-four-hour basis. Tell them it's a top-priority emergency and get them over here stat."

"All right," Kit whispered and headed for the reception room to carry out his request.

"You shouldn't have come, Lucy. For the sake of the children, I'll give you an hour, no more. Go upstairs and gather them up. We'll eat at the Village Inn."

"Oh, Jarod!"

Kit could hear their conversation clearly and thought the other woman sounded shattered.

"I'd hoped we could stay the whole day. I planned to help you get settled in. We drove all this way in the snow just to see you. The children brought more things to decorate their room."

"You should have told me you were coming."

"I left messages but you didn't return my calls."

"That's because I've been busy with patients. Next time, wait for an invitation so the children won't be disappointed. It was sheer luck that Linda was here to let you in.''

"Then let me have a key."

"This is a clinic as well as my home. Everything works on the remote when I'm not here, making it impossible for you to get in."

"Surely you can spare another remote for your family."

"Not if I want to retain my license to keep drugs here."

"Oh, Jarod. Let's not quarrel. I've missed you so much."

Kit heard raw pain in Lucy Banning's voice and it racked her with guilt as she kept trying to reach the glass company, whose line continued to be busy. Obviously, Dr. Banning's stern reaction to his sister-in-law's unexpected arrival had everything to do with Kit's presence beneath his roof. In attempting to keep it a secret, he risked alienating his brother's wife and disappointing the niece and nephew he patently adored.

It occurred to Kit that the two of them might be closer than brother and sister-in-law. In fact, it was more than possible, as Kit knew from personal experience. After all, she and Ross had been dating when he met Laura and married her....

Maybe Dr. Banning had been in love with Lucy for a long time. Maybe he'd never been able to bring himself to marry anyone else because of his attraction to her. She *was* lovely. Maybe...

Kit let out a tortured moan and castigated herself for letting her thoughts run wild. Whatever their relationship, it was none of her business. Two days ago, she'd never heard of Dr. Jarod Banning.

Had Laura been right when she suggested that Kit craved attention now that their father was gone? To feel this proprietorial about a man Kit had known less than two days bordered on the irrational. She had to snap out of it!

"That's quite a conversation you're having with yourself," Dr. Banning observed from the opposite side of her desk.

She felt her face go hot, wondering how long he'd been standing there while she carried on her inner battle. "I'm sorry that my being here has caused problems for you."

His dark glance withered her on the spot. "Stop apologizing. You've done everything exactly right and your disguise is so perfect, I'm having a hard time believing Kit Mitchell lives at this address."

Kit shook her head. "You don't have to be kind to me, Dr. Banning. I realize what helping me is costing you, and I do have to apologize," she went on, talking as if he hadn't spoken. "I'm afraid my presence is going to cause more complications than either of us anticipated."

He stiffened. "Lucy blundered her way in here and caused the complication, Kit."

"But she has the right. She's family."

His features hardened. "Which makes what she did worse because she knows better than to disturb me without making prior arrangements, especially now that I spend the bulk of my time in Salt Lake.

I'm taking steps to make certain it doesn't happen again. Have you reached the glass company?''

"Not yet.''

"Keep trying. I'll be back within the hour.''

Seconds later, his sister-in-law and her children came down the stairs, and Dr. Banning formally introduced Chet and Jennifer to Linda, his new receptionist, before they left for lunch.

As the front door closed, Kit heard Jennifer ask, "If Chet broke the window, why did you say Mom would have to pay for it, Uncle Jarod?''

"I was thinking out loud, Jennifer. Grown-ups sometimes do.''

CHAPTER FOUR

WORK. Kit needed work. Anything to get her mind off the man who was fast becoming her obsession. Unfortunately, hearing Dr. Banning's voice while she was transcribing one of his tapes made it impossible to think about anyone else.

Worse, when she finally did reach the glass company and a man was sent out, she had to stay upstairs in Dr. Banning's bedroom while he replaced the window. Not even the distraction of the television helped.

After the workman left, she sat on a chair and finished watching the world news, but she only half listened to reports about another earthquake in northern Italy and more scandal within the royal family. Right now, her world was confined to the walls of this house and she felt separated from any other reality.

Until she saw a picture of herself flashed on the screen as the local news began.

It was the same photograph that had appeared in every newspaper sold throughout Utah. Kit watched mesmerized as the anchorman repeated what had been written about her by the press.

"At this time, police speculate Ms. Mitchell has been abducted, possibly by extortionists who

57

hope to obtain a ransom for her safe return. It is estimated that her deceased father, William Mitchell, left an estate worth over a million dollars to the victim and her sister, Laura Mitchell Hunter, wife of Ross Hunter, of Mitchell, Hunter and Associates.

"Since her disappearance from the Capitol Theater two nights ago, Salt Lake Police are investigating all rumors, particularly those circulating among friends closest to Ms. Mitchell that she has been depressed since the death of her father and over the past few months has exhibited signs of breaking under the strain.

"Our station is standing by to flash pictures of the victim on the screen. If you have seen this woman, please call the number at the bott—"

In a rage, Kit flew at the television and turned it off, absolutely livid. "I have *not* been depressed," she cried out in agony and flung herself across the bed, sobbing.

"Kit?"

Startled, she rolled over on her back and sat up. "I—I'm sorry, Dr. Banning. I was watching television and the news upset me," she said, struggling to hold back a sob.

"So I gather."

Embarrassed to have been caught in such a vulnerable state, she tried to get away, but he prevented any movement by sitting down next to her and pulling her into his arms, holding her head against his solid chest.

"If you're going to cry, then let's at least get rid of the wig or I'll have to buy you another one tomorrow."

With deft fingers, he removed the blond wig and put it on the nearby chair. Kit was so grateful for the warmth and touch of another human body, she didn't question the gesture and nestled deeply in his arms, finding comfort in the steady beat of his heart against her cheek.

"Let's talk about what upset you most," he suggested quietly.

With sobs racking her body, it was difficult to unburden herself, and it was humiliating because her tears were soaking his sweater even though he seemed oblivious.

"The man said that everyone closest to me thought I'd had a nervous b-breakdown, intimating that I'm unstable. Obviously, no one believed me about the messages. Laura's not the only one to think that I made everything up, that I planted the notes myself."

"How does that make you feel?"

"Like my whole life is invalid, that none of my past relationships with people have ever counted."

"But *you* know the truth and can forgive all of those people who love you and feel utterly helpless. They're searching for *any* explanation to explain your disappearance."

As his wisdom sank in, Kit felt considerably better and eventually the tears stopped. After a while, she lifted her head from its warm resting place so redolent of his own enticing body scent and after-shave. Suddenly aware of his close proximity, she moved away and stood up, wiping her eyes.

"Thank you for telling me that."

He rose to his feet. "I believe in you, Kit."

"*Thank God*," she whispered.

"Go fix yourself something to eat. As soon as I've dealt with a few phone calls, come to my office. I want to talk to you."

By the time he left the bedroom, she could hardly breathe and rushed to the kitchen to get herself under control. She hadn't wanted to leave his arms at all.

He'd known instinctively that she needed physical comfort and it would be wrong to read anything more into what had happened. But if she ever found herself in the same position again, she might not be able to keep from raising her lips to his.

An unbidden image of Lucy Banning doing just that caused Kit to wield the carving knife too carelessly. She cut her finger while slicing the ham and had to run cold water over the wound. It brought her ruminations to a halt.

She used a paper napkin to stop the bleeding, then ate her sandwich and hurried through the house to his office.

"Step into my parlor," he said on a dry note as Kit appeared in the doorway, eyeing the tape recorder warily. There was no question which role he was playing at the moment.

"You were relaxed upstairs. Now you've gone all stiff on me. Dart would like some background information on you, which we're going to do our best to supply. If you'd prefer to lie down on the couch, go right ahead.''

"Doctors don't use couches. I read it in a book."

"Don't believe everything you read. Couches have their uses."

"I don't think I'll comment on that."

His deep chuckle resonated through every cell of her body. She'd never been more aware of a man's virile appeal and tried to look elsewhere so she wouldn't be distracted.

"What was it like growing up in the Mitchell family?"

"What was it like?" she whispered.

He nodded. "How did your family function?"

"Well—Daddy was always a very busy person. If I hoped to spend time with him, I had to figure out ways to accomplish it, so I usually went on his morning walks with him.''

"Your mother didn't go?"

"No. Mother was sick a lot. She died of cancer when I was nineteen. Daddy was devoted to her and our family suffered a great deal during that period.

"After her death, I presume he needed even more of a physical outlet, so he put in a pool and started swimming. Until his fatal heart attack, we usually walked or swam before he left for work in the morning.''

"Did your sister join you?"

"Occasionally. But Laura's favorite time to be with Dad was at the office. They ate lunch together several times a week."

"When did your father die?"

Her smile faded. "About eighteen months ago."

He pursed his lips. "Did all your physical activities stop at that point?"

"No. After Dad was gone, Laura and Ross came to live at the house so I wouldn't be alone. But I wanted to be on my own, so I moved to a condo in town. There's a swimming pool I use most mornings before I go to work."

One dark brow quirked. "Do others swim with you?"

"Yes."

"Anyone in particular?"

"No. Well, there used to be someone."

"Who?"

"Chris Holloway. For almost a year, we swam laps together."

"Male or female?"

"Male. He's a nineteen-year-old sophomore at the university."

"Was he an acquaintance or a friend?"

"A friend, definitely. We grew quite close, although I haven't seen him lately, of course."

There was a slight pause before Dr. Banning said, "Did you see him on other occasions besides swimming?"

"Yes. There was a time when he used to come to my condo to talk. His parents divorced when he started college and he was in a lot of pain."

"Dart will want to know all about him. You never received one of those threatening notes while you were with Chris?"

She sobered. "No."

"Do you eat breakfast in or out?"

"I usually cook a big one after my swim. Once I'm at work, I tend to forget everything else."

"You said 'usually'. What are the exceptions?"

"Sometimes Laura and Ross invite me for Sunday brunch. But for the most part, I like to stay home on the weekend and run my projects on the computer."

He sat foward in the chair. "You've given me a rough idea of your family and your activities. Now I want to talk for a minute about relationships. Let's start with Chris. How do you feel about him?"

She frowned. "What do you mean?"

"Are your feelings friendly, sisterly, romantic?"

"*Romantic—Chris*?" she scoffed. "Hardly. But I suppose I feel a little of all those other emotions you mentioned. He's rather unsure of himself. But he's a wonderful person, and someday when he's found himself, he's going to be a power to reckon with and he'll end up breaking lots of hearts."

"When he tells you how beautiful you are, what do you say?"

"That someday, someone is going to believe him, and he'll be in big trouble."

"And when he doesn't want to leave your condo, how do you handle it?"

"I tell him we're both hardworking people and need an early night."

"When he shows his appreciation and gives you a hug and a kiss on the cheek, are you repulsed by him?"

"Of course not."

"When he first gave you a man's kiss, did that change anything?"

She blinked. "No! Because I saw it coming and stopped letting him in after that."

Kit remembered the hurt look on his face when he'd begged her to let him stay over. The longing in his expression had given him away. He hadn't joined her for a swim since.

By some magic, Dr. Banning had forced her to remember that night and had elicited information from her so deeply buried, she'd forgotten about it until this moment. Kit looked at him through new eyes and sat forward, her hands interlocked over her knee.

"*How did you do that*?" she asked in awe.

He grinned. "In court, it's called leading the witness. I'm surprised the daughter of such a noted attorney doesn't know that."

"Dad always said I had a one-track mind."

"How fortunate for Stragi-Corp," he murmured dryly. "But getting back to our conversation... From a totally impartial point of view, can you see that Chris Holloway could be a suspect?

"He's been spurned by a beautiful, brilliant woman not much older than himself, who has given him a sense of self-worth, built his self-esteem, provided companionship. And suddenly, she's cut him off. Depending on his emotional stability and a host of other factors, he could be your stalker.''

Kit sat there in astonishment. ''I would never have considered him, let alone in that light.''

''Probably not. The point is, you may not think of him, but it's painfully obvious that Chris Holloway thinks he's in love with you. You're all he has on his mind, and since you rejected him, he's probably in considerable pain. You might even have become an obsession.''

She bowed her head. ''It can't be Chris. I don't want to believe it.''

''But at least now you know he's a possibility.''

''Yes.''

''How do you feel about Jeremy?''

She groaned. ''I don't think I'm up to this.''

''No one ever is.''

''Could we talk about him another time?''

''Dart needs this information right away.''

''I'm sorry.'' She shook her head. ''I don't know what's wrong with me.''

''Your reaction is entirely normal. The closer we come to the heart of the matter, the more you'll fight. It's a simple defense mechanism, making you feel cross and out of sorts. Releasing suppressed emotions is painful.''

She took a deep breath. ''My feelings for Jeremy aren't that different from the ones I have for Chris.''

''Except that there's a rumor floating at your company that you and he are lovers, and that's the reason you got the job over two hundred other male applicants.''

Kit was on her feet in an instant, her eyes angry green licks of flame. "How did you come by that gossip? Because that's all it is."

"The information is common knowledge according to Dart, who already had his ear to the ground on your case before I called him."

"It's a lie. I swear it."

"Which part?" he coaxed softly, not moving a muscle.

His question caught her on the raw. "He wants to be more than friends, but I don't. As for sleeping with him, it's not worthy of an answer."

"Because it's Ross Hunter you've been sleeping with?"

Her face blanched. "Was that in the police report, too?"

He pursed his lips. "Have you been intimate with your brother-in-law? Someone seems to think so."

"I've never been to bed with a man," she confessed quietly. "If I had, it would probably have been with the Swedish graduate student who taught my physics class. Thankfully, I found out in time that he had something going with a female in every class he taught. So I started flirting with a friend of his who also worked for the department, which wounded his colossal ego, and that was the end of it."

Dr. Banning's head bent back in laughter.

She smiled at the sound. "You may think it's ridiculous, but he said all the right things to enchant my romantic soul and he *was* a rather astounding male specimen."

Kit covertly eyed the attractive man seated across from her, realizing that no other man she'd ever met or known could compare with him.

"Is he the only person to have captured your imagination, if not your heart?"

She sucked in her breath, wondering what he'd say if she told him *he* held those exclusive honors.

"The only other person who even came close was Ross when he first joined Dad's firm. In the beginning, I was totally infatuated with him like every other woman. He was eight years older and very suave."

"Was this before or after your Swede?"

"After." She put her palms up in front of him. "And I know what you're going to say. That I was ready to fall into Ross's arms like the proverbial plum and you would be right. I heard all this from Daddy, who made sure I kept my feet on the ground until I could figure things out with my head as well as my heart. By that time, he'd met Laura and they were married soon after."

"Did you date Ross?"

"For a very short time."

"Yet he ended up with Laura?"

"Yes. He liked me, but when he met Laura, it was love at first sight."

"You just stepped out of the way?"

"It wasn't like that."

"Then how was it?"

"When Ross wanted a more intimate relationship, I pulled back. At first he was upset, then apologized. We parted friends. Not long after that, he started seeing Laura.''

"Didn't that bother you?''

"It would have if I'd been in love with him in the first place. But since I'd never felt that way about him, it didn't matter, not when I could see how crazy they were about each other. Daddy and I both commented on it.''

"Nevertheless, rumors can have some basis in fact. It's possible that Ross never got over you. Maybe since the miscarriage, Laura doesn't attract him right now. Sometimes depression can shut a man out when he needs his wife most. Maybe he's always been secretly in love with you because he never possessed you, and now you're all that fills his vision. Maybe he wrote those notes to manipulate you.''

"Stop it, Jarod!'' she cried out in panic, then blushed because she'd forgotten to call him Dr. Banning.

His eyes flared with interest. "I wondered when you'd start calling me by my first name,'' he murmured. "Why the outrage, Kit? Did I hit a little too close to home? After all, you went back to live with Ross and Laura before you ran away.''

Defeated, she mumbled, "I know.''

"Has Laura accused you of being unfaithful with her husband behind her back? After all, he met you first.''

Unable to take any more, Kit buried her face in her hands and couldn't prevent her shoulders from shaking as the tears came.

"Has Ross been sending out signals? Answer me!"

After a prolonged silence, Kit whispered, "I'm not sure."

"And what has been your response?"

Slowly, she lifted her head and faced him. "Inwardly, I've been appalled. Outwardly, I've pretended that I didn't notice."

"Because of your loyalty to Laura?"

"Because of that and because I'm not in love with him!" she avowed. "When I first met him, I was young and in love with love. But I outgrew that. If he still wants me, then he's a fool, and all I feel is disgust."

"Have you considered that Jeremy, whom you've already turned down, might sense a rival and feel threatened?"

"Not until now." Her voice held a distinct tremor.

"Have you ever looked at him as a man?"

"No. We work so closely together, I can't see him in any other capacity than as my boss. Besides, does a person ever really know another person? He's fifteen years older than I am and he already has one failed marriage behind him. I'd be afraid to get involved with him, even if I wanted to. When I finally make a decision about a man, it's going to be irreversible."

"Irreversible?"

"If and when I marry, I'll stay married. Period."

"Like your parents?"

"Yes."

"If you could describe your father in one sentence, how would you do it?"

"That's easy," she said, smiling despite the tears. "He was a total man, complete in every way." *Like you, Jarod Banning.*

"Because he gave you everything you wanted? Some people might see it that way, accuse him of spoiling you."

His comment devastated her.

"No! Because he was good and kind and honest. Because he put Mother's happiness above his own and was the most selfless man I ever knew." She paused. "If he had a flaw, it was probably the fact that he worked so hard. But that was because he was in so much pain. He didn't know how to play like other men. He preferred to come home in the evenings and be with Mom. I never heard him malign another human being or talk about money."

Jarod got to his feet and turned off the recorder. "And every man who has ever wanted a relationship with you knows instinctively that he'll never measure up to your father. A cold, cruel fact of life that could turn a would-be lover into a psychopath." He started toward her.

The room reverberated with his summation.

"Dr. Banning—" she finally began in a low voice.

"Jarod," he corrected her with a smile, "except when we're around patients."

"Jarod—" she mouthed his name under her breath "—is that really the way I come across to you?"

His hand squeezed her shoulder. "Not at all. You have to understand that what we've accomplished tonight has had a twofold purpose. To let Dart inside your head, and to take the veil from your eyes where others might be concerned."

Her face closed up. "You're the expert. You said your aim was to make me see myself through another person's eyes and you've done it. I'm not sure I like what I see."

"I like what I see very much." His hand tightened briefly before letting her go. "The point is, if I can get you to be a little more objective about yourself, *you* may be the one who solves your own case, given enough time."

A shudder ran through her body. "I'm tired."

"I'm not surprised. You've provided me with enough material to keep Dart busy until Wednesday night when we'll have another talk."

"I don't think I could go through this again," she replied and stood up on trembling legs. "I've told you everything I know."

His eyes narrowed. "We've only scratched the surface. It's necessary to explore your relationships with women next."

Her mind went blank. "Why?"

"Hasn't it occurred to you that a woman might be responsible for attempting to drive you over the brink?"

"A woman?" she questioned, aghast.

"Obviously it hasn't," he muttered. "Think about it when you go to bed tonight. Use the same devices we employed just now. Construct scenarios that could fit. You know how to do it. The results might astound you.''

She went dizzy for a moment and grabbed hold of the chair.

"Sit down, Kit.''

She did his bidding, feeling too weak to move. "I'm frightened,'' she whispered.

He strode from the room and came back seconds later, handing her a glass of brandy. "Drink it. All of it.''

The liquid burned its way down her throat to her stomach. Almost immediately, the warmth soothed her nerves. "I—I've got to go to bed.'' She rose from the chair and moved to the doorway, then turned to him. "I realize I should thank you, but somehow I can't bring myself to do it. Good night.''

"Good night, Kit. Please don't hesitate to disturb me if you need to talk later.'' Beneath his words, she sensed intense emotion but didn't know what it signified.

The next twelve hours opened up to Kit like a yawning chasm. Jarod was an extraordinary person to effectively penetrate her psyche like that. She'd revealed disjointed bits of information, which when pieced together began to form patterns that made a strange kind of sense.

She knew that the prerequisite for a good internist was the ability to weigh all the physical evidence and come up with the right diagnosis. Jarod also possessed an uncanny ability to force thought from her subconscious. One talk with him and the layers had been peeled away.

She cried until there were no more tears to cry. One thing had become crystal clear. Because she hero-worshipped her father, she'd kept men at a distance all her life, even Ross. That was the reason it hadn't damaged her when he discovered Laura.

The truth was that right from the start Ross had fallen short, displaying a selfish streak that meant he would always put himself first in a relationship. Since her father was the exact opposite, Kit had chosen to steer clear of Ross.

But her sister had different needs altogether and closed her eyes to Ross's self-absorption, with the result that she and Ross had fought a lot throughout their marriage because they both wanted their own way in everything. Kit hadn't taken any of it very seriously, but it had been a factor in her wanting to get a place of her own.

Fighting seemed so foreign to her when she could scarcely remember a cross word between her mother and father. They'd always been so eager to please, so willing to put their own needs aside for the sake of the other.

Her thoughts shifted to Jeremy. He was a genius in his field and a great wit. It made him exciting to work for and forced Kit to stretch mentally. But no matter how he tried to hide it, a sadness lurked behind his ready smile.

She had an idea he grieved for his wife, though he denied the fact vehemently. It occurred to Kit that he needed some counseling. Until he got it, she couldn't take him seriously. No woman could.

Somehow, she couldn't see Jeremy as her stalker. He had other demons to exorcize. Nor could she imagine Ross as the culprit. Ross loved himself too much to allow a woman to dominate his thoughts.

She turned on her side and puffed up the pillow. That left Chris Holloway, an unhappy young man trying to be an adult in a world turned upside down by his parents' divorce. She couldn't see him being responsible for those hideous notes. Hurt pride didn't necessarily produce a psychopath.

As for the other men she'd dated at the university and more recently at work, those relationships hadn't developed into anything of substance because—because they just hadn't...

The most intimate thing she'd ever done in her life was spend the past two days and nights with Jarod Banning.

She'd followed his suggestion and made a list of possible suspects—people with whom she associated at work. Kit included those acquaintances at the condo, as well, but after turning these possibilities over in her mind, she didn't believe any one of them harbored sufficient feelings of animosity or desire to perpetrate such a cruel plan.

What haunted her now was the realization that other than her mother and Laura, Kit hadn't cultivated many deep-seated relationships with women.

Because their mom had been an invalid for so long, Kit and Laura had worked out a schedule to wait on her. As a result, neither of them had had a lot of time for girlfriends. Like their father, everything revolved around their mom.

Kit kept in touch with a few teenage friends, but her closest female relationship outside the family had been with the wonderful nurse taking care of her mother at the end. Kit couldn't conceive of that woman being her stalker.

She stared at the ceiling, still feeling the sting of the newscaster's words. Maybe she *had* been in a depression since her father died and everyone had noticed it except her. But she hadn't fabricated those notes. Thank God Jarod believed her!

Jarod.

She hugged the pillow, aware of another kind of fear creeping into her heart, a fear that had nothing at all to do with those terrifying notes.

CHAPTER FIVE

"GOOD morning, Ms. Smith."

Jarod entered the reception room dressed in an expensive-looking, tailored blue suit. The tiny blue stripes of his white shirt and silk tie added a more formal touch and Kit experienced a violent physical reaction when she looked up at him.

After her dreams of last night, she had trouble suppressing the waves of longing his nearness evoked. In only a short time, he'd become vital to her existence and she couldn't help drinking in his handsome features, the way his brown hair curled on his neck still damp from the shower. His eyes . . .

Before she lost her wits, she blurted, "Good morning, Dr. Banning. Your first appointment is here."

"I noticed." His gaze darted to three patients who'd come in at the same time. Inclining his head, he said, "I have a luncheon engagement at noon but I'll be back in time for my two o'clock appointment. After my last patient, you can gather up the tapes and transcribe them. I won't be in for dinner so you can please yourself."

Her face fell in disappointment. She masked it by asking, "If there's an emergency, what should I do?"

"I'll leave the name of a colleague on my desk. He covers for me when I'm not on call."

She tried to keep her tone neutral. "When can I expect you back?"

"Probably ten-thirty or so. Any other questions?"

A little devil of amusement lurked around his mouth. He knew how strange and new this situation had to be for her, particularly in front of patients.

"Your sister-in-law said something about a Mrs. Baxter."

At the mention of Lucy Banning, he sobered. "Did she ask if you were my cleaning lady's replacement?"

"I guess she assumed it."

A look she couldn't decipher crossed his features. "Mrs. Baxter comes in at five, Monday through Friday. Let her in the front door. She'll clean while you finish up the paperwork and make phone calls."

"And where will you be?" She eyed him suspiciously.

"Out."

"I see."

"Why else do you think I hired you if not to run interference?"

Laugh lines formed grooves at either side of his mouth. He ought to do it more often, she mused, out of breath by now.

"Come in, Mr. Welch," he said, speaking up to be heard. "How did that new medication work?"

The old man went into a long spiel about how much better he felt and shuffled past Kit's desk. Jarod gave him his full attention, displaying a remarkable bedside manner, which Kit knew from experience was missing in many doctors.

One by one, patients came and went. After lunch, Kit found herself listening with compassion to a mother whose child had developed ulcers because she was afraid the school building would catch on fire. But until Jarod had used his incomparable methods to get the truth out of her daughter, no one, not even the girl's pediatrician, had been able to make sense of the trauma that prevented her from stepping outside her house every morning.

The last patient of the afternoon had been diagnosed with cancer. His spouse sat out with Kit and talked nonstop about Dr. Banning being a savior, how he'd found the disease in time to give her husband a few more years of life.

Kit's admiration for Jarod's ability to deal with each situation and still retain a sense of humor amazed her. Before she knew it, the day was gone and she found herself typing up notes.

The cleaning lady was nice enough, though she talked a trifle too much about Jarod, whom she obviously adored. Kit could understand Lucy Banning's remark a little better now. Starting the next day, Kit determined to be on the phone while Mrs. Baxter did her job, and every day after that, if necessary.

Contrary to Kit's belief that she'd miss her work at Stragi-Corp, Jarod's busy schedule set a precedent for the rest of the week and Kit never gave her old job a thought.

After hours, she experimented on recipes in the kitchen and made up several casseroles she could freeze so Jarod would have something hot for lunch.

An emergency on Wednesday night prevented Kit from spending another emotional session with Jarod. In one sense, she felt relief that she wouldn't be forced to delve into the awful task of figuring out who hated her enough to try to drive her out of her mind.

On the other hand, Kit craved time alone with him and coveted even a quickly shared meal between appointments. It seemed like weeks instead of days since they'd had blocks of undisturbed time together.

On Jarod's advice, she didn't go outside, and she refrained from reading the newspaper or watching the news on television. Anything she heard or read had to be speculation on the media's part and would serve no purpose but to distress her.

Kit complied with his suggestion, seeing the wisdom in isolating herself from innuendo. It could only cause unnecessary pain. Instead, when she went to bed, she immersed herself in a couple of historical novels. Jarod had picked them up for her along with the groceries when he went to the supermarket.

However, by Friday morning, the walls had started to close in on her and she looked forward to the drive to Heber. Finally, she'd get Jarod to herself. The thought filled her with so much excitement, she thought she was running a temperature.

While she waited impatiently for his last appointment to leave the office, the phone rang and she recognized Lucy Banning's voice.

Kit's heart sank when she realized she wasn't the only person wanting Jarod's undivided attention. It brought her down to earth with a vengeance.

Traveling to the mountains in the car with Jarod might be the only time they would have alone. Lucy Banning and the children had a prior claim to his love, a fact she couldn't afford to forget.

She buzzed Jarod and told him his sister-in-law was on the line. He gave her instructions to have Lucy hold, that he'd be with her shortly.

When Kit remembered Jarod's air of excitement earlier that morning, a pain shot through her as real as a knife piercing her insides. He couldn't wait to get back to his ranch!

Was he in love with Lucy?

The mere idea sent Kit into a depression of a different kind. She simply didn't know how to deal with the emotions running rampant through her body. She'd never been in love before....

"A penny for them," Jarod whispered near her ear, and immediately she was flooded by a yielding feeling of delight. He'd seen his last patient to the door and had started whistling tunelessly as he gave a cursory glance to some correspondence she'd left for him to read. "Let's get out of here, Linda Smith. It's time to play."

"I'll finish packing," Kit murmured and hurried upstairs. Since Tuesday, the guest bedroom had been hers, complete with a new bed, dresser, bedside table and lamp that Jarod had had delivered.

"Ready? I'll take your bags down to the car."

He walked into her bedroom, casually dressed in well-worn Levi's that molded to his powerful legs, a dark gray pullover and his sheepskin coat.

"Yes. I'm all set."

She, too, had dressed informally in one of the pairs of jeans he'd bought for her, which she toned with the cream-colored sweater.

"I gave Mrs. Baxter the leftover food from the refrigerator. I hated to see it go to waste and couldn't think of anything else to do." When he didn't say anything and continued to stare at her, she started to grow nervous. "I—I've decided to wear the wig and glasses. The remote possibility that someone might identify me never leaves my mind."

"I think that's wise," he murmured, again sounding far away. She feared he was thinking about Lucy and it set her heart thudding. "Although we've had a string of people in and out of the office all week and no one has had a clue," he added quietly.

She sucked in her breath. "There was one small problem with Mr. Laird. He likes to talk to me on the phone. I don't want to be rude to him but—"

"I'm aware of his interest," Jarod grated. "He's called me twice about a prescription, when in reality he was pumping me for information about my gorgeous blond receptionist.''

"But he's in the middle of a nasty divorce suit!"

"Now we know why."

Kit felt the heat creep into her face. "W-what did you tell him about me?"

"That my staff is off limits, that he'd do best to concentrate on his peptic ulcer. Period. He got the message." Jarod sounded almost possessive and it sent a thrill through her body.

She shut the overnight bag he'd purchased for her. "I finished typing your notes. This week's histories are complete."

Jarod's masculine presence seemed to fill the room. "I haven't really had an opportunity before now to tell you what an outstanding job you've done as my receptionist and secretary. Your company's loss is my gain," he quipped. "Depending on what Dart has planned, I'd like you to help at the clinic in Heber in your spare time."

Kit's head flew back in surprise.

"My brother and I shared a receptionist," Jarod went on to explain, "but after he died, I urged her to find another position. Lucy has been filling in temporarily, but she doesn't know how to type. I've a backlog of tapes to be transcribed and prefer to use you."

Kit put on her new coat and reached for her handbag. "Mightn't she resent someone else taking over?"

"She won't be happy about it, but the decision isn't hers to make. I let Lucy come into the office on a part-time basis after Grayson died to keep her occupied until she could begin to cope. The time is long past due for her to become involved in something more in keeping with her interests and talents. Within three months, I'll be practicing full-time in Salt Lake anyway.

"Once Dart discovers who's been stalking you and he's put behind bars, I'll lose you to Stragi-Corp. When that day comes, I'll train someone with a nursing background for a permanent position," he explained as they went down the stairs.

Kit almost stumbled and had to grab the banister for support. She felt like she'd just been stabbed in the heart again. While she'd been living in a kind of fool's paradise, weaving fantasies about Jarod, he'd been planning his future, his mind already light-years ahead.

Kit listened intently as she checked her wig in the hall mirror one more time before they walked out back to the garage. No matter what Jarod said, Lucy Banning had other plans and she'd be positively livid when Kit showed up with him.

In fact, if it looked as though she was coming between the two of them, Kit determined to find another place to hide out while Mr. Thueson worked on her case. Her arrival on Jarod's doorstep had plunged them into unforeseen complications. Kit absolutely refused to cause him any more trouble.

The sun fell below the horizon as he maneuvered his green Land Rover through the slushy, crowded, downtown streets to the freeway.

"I'd like to take you out to dinner, but for obvious reasons, I think we'd better eat in the car. How does that sound?"

"I'm relieved, actually. Since I met you, I've felt so safe and I want that to continue. After a week's confinement, it's wonderful just being in the car."

"Once we're in Heber, you can relax and take long walks in the snow along the country lanes."

"Sounds like heaven," she murmured, imagining the two of them wrapped in each other's arms, braving the elements.

"I'm aware the atmosphere at the office has been claustrophobic. You must feel like you're escaping from prison."

"I'm not complaining," she hastened to assure him. "Where exactly do you have your practice?"

Jarod turned onto the interstate. "In an office building on the main street of town. The ranch house is on the outskirts of Heber. Lucy and the children own it now. After Grayson died, I moved to the bunkhouse, which I share with Skip, my foreman, and a couple of the hands."

Kit could imagine how Lucy felt about that! "Is it a large ranch?" Anything to get her mind off his sister-in-law.

Jarod flicked her a penetrating glance. "Ten thousand acres isn't very big, but it sustains enough cattle to turn a decent profit."

"How do you manage to be a doctor and run a ranch at the same time?"

"I don't. The hands do the heavy work. I just play at it in my spare time."

She felt him smile in the semidarkness and it made her happy. "Does your ranch have a name like the Lazy Z or some such thing?"

"My dad named it the High Rustler."

"After the ski run in Alta?"

"That's right."

"Were *you* a skier as well as a rancher?"

Kit turned in her seat so she could watch him while he drove. The flash of headlights revealed the uncompromising lines and angles of his unforgettable face.

When he didn't say anything, she prodded gently, "I notice that you didn't answer my question, but there's no hurry. Perhaps in our next session we'll get inside Jarod Banning's psyche and discover that even a doctor isn't immune to the problems that beset mere mortals."

For the next fifteen minutes, total quiet enveloped them. Whether by design or coincidence, Jarod eventually turned off on the Park City road and drove them to a fast-food restaurant.

Explaining that he wouldn't be long, he levered himself out of the Rover and covered the distance to the entrance in a few long strides. He kept the engine running so she would have the benefit of the heater.

Kit rested her head against the icy-cold window, hating the stiffness of the wig. She'd gone too far with Jarod. Evidently his past was off-limits. She'd been a fool to pry into his private life and berated herself for assuming she had the right to put their relationship on anything other than a professional footing.

If only they could have met under different circumstances. Being in his debt changed the complexion of the whole situation, forcing her to be aware of what she said and how she behaved. She didn't like it. In fact, her attraction to him threatened to overpower all other considerations.

Shortly, Jarod returned to the car with their dinner. As soon as he got in and shut the door, he turned to her. They both spoke each other's name at the same time.

Kit's nervous laugh broke the tension. "I only wanted to say that I'm sorry if I offended you earlier, Jarod. Please forgive me."

He pulled a cheeseburger from the sack and handed it to her with a napkin. "There's nothing to forgive." He reversed the car, taking a bite of his dinner before driving onto the main highway once more.

Traffic had thinned considerably. By the time they took the turnoff for Heber, he could accelerate without difficulty and the Land Rover fairly flew over the freshly plowed highway.

"I met my wife skiing when we were teenagers." Upon hearing those words, Kit's heart plummeted to her feet. "We married out of high school. She had a dream to go to the Olympics because she was that good. But an avalanche paralyzed her from the waist down.

"With each unsuccessful operation, she fell into a deeper depression. When she learned she could never be intimate with me again, could never have children, she decided to put an end to her torment in the only way she knew how."

Kit was stunned. She didn't know what to say. Her food tasted like sawdust. "I—I'm sorry, Jarod. I had no right to make you remember something so painful."

He drained the contents of his drink. "Stop apologizing, Kit. It's your worst trait. Frankly, I'm glad the subject came up so there are no secrets," he said in a calm voice. "Amy will always be a bittersweet memory because she gave up on our marriage. *In sickness and in health*, the line goes."

"She couldn't have been in her right mind when she did that, Jarod."

"Maybe. Maybe not. Obviously, the will to live must come from within. I gave her all the support possible, but ultimately she was free to choose life or death."

With bent head, Kit said, "I'm beginning to understand why you didn't pressure me to stay with you. Force doesn't work," she theorized aloud.

"I didn't need to force you, Kit. You're a fighter and chose to stay and face your fear instead of running off to Nevada and who knows what other horrors. That's why I'm finding such pleasure in helping you."

The explanation about his wife answered a big question in her mind concerning his fundamental motive for playing the Good Samaritan.

It also broke her heart. While she'd been entertaining personal and intimate thoughts of him, he'd been using Kit to fulfill a need that his wife had denied him.

"I haven't been in pain where she's concerned since I went away to medical school years ago," he continued, oblivious to her agony. "But there are friends of mine in Heber who persist in believing that I'm still secretly grieving. Now that you know the truth, you'll be better equipped to deal with gossip. Small towns thrive on it."

"So do big cities," Kit interjected with feeling.

Jarod reached in the sack for another burger. "What is your fee for this session, Dr. Mitchell?"

His use of her last name made her face go hot. "I don't charge my friends."

"You don't need the money."

"That was true before I landed on your doorstep."

"Tell me." He turned toward her. "How long has it been since you totally relaxed?"

She felt his gaze but no longer wondered which person had asked the question. His feelings for her had never been anything but that of a doctor for a supplicant who needed healing.

"I don't remember. I've had too many worries for too long."

"Then let's do something about that. Tomorrow, as soon as Dart has finished with you, we'll hitch up the horses and I'll take you on a long sleigh ride."

A few minutes ago, she would have cried out with excitement, her heart exploding in her chest because they'd be spending the whole day together, alone.

"Only if you can spare the time," she replied, struggling to keep her voice from wobbling. "I haven't done that since I was little."

If he noticed a change in her, he didn't let it show. "It'll get cold and we'll be isolated. Does that bother you?"

"Of course not. I'll be with you," she said without thinking, then quickly averted her eyes.

"That's nice to hear. I wish I could inspire that kind of trust in all my patients."

Her happiness had flown out the window. In its place, anger flared briefly. She didn't want him treating her like one of his patients. She wanted to mean much more to him than that!

Did all his female patients suffer from the same affliction? How many women had imagined themselves in love with him before now? An occupational hazard?

But Kit wasn't his patient, not in the accepted sense of the word, and she hadn't been imagining the feelings that had been growing since that first night when he examined her in his clinic.

They both saw twinkling lights in the distance at the same time. "We'll be home inside of five minutes," Jarod confirmed.

Home.

The sound of it in connection with Jarod intensified the ache gnawing inside her. While she sat there in turmoil, they drove the rest of the way in silence. As they passed through the heart of town, he slowed down long enough to point out his office located in a two-story brick building near the local movie theater. Then they reached the outskirts.

Jarod turned left off the highway onto a road leading past snow-covered fields dotted by an occasional farmhouse. Before long, Kit could make out the immaculately kept ranch house.

It resembled a huge three-story red barn with one-story wings attached at either side and connected by a black sloping roof where the words "High Rustler" were painted in white letters.

Two enormous pine trees in the front were decorated with thousands of colored lights left over from the holidays. The whole scene belonged on a Christmas card.

Even before Jarod pulled up in front, two golden retrievers came dashing across the snow, barking in obvious excitement because their master was home.

"That's odd," he muttered. "The children are always with them."

"Maybe they're glued to a TV show and didn't hear the dogs barking."

Jarod didn't look convinced, but he dropped the subject. "As soon as we get inside, I'll make a fire in the kitchen and we'll put some steaks on the grill. Those hamburgers hardly made a dent in my appetite."

Kit had to clamp down hard on her joy. Though she wouldn't be losing Jarod tonight, she could never forget that this was Lucy's home and it was about to be invaded.

The air froze her lungs as he opened her door and helped her to the ground, warning Fred and Zelda to behave. But Kit didn't mind them licking her. Like all animals, they were curious and she fell in love with them right away.

They danced around her as she moved toward the entrance. The snow crunched beneath her feet and she could see her breath while she waited for Jarod to open the door.

The foyer reminded her of an inviting dude ranch, everything made of white oak with colorful rag rugs on the hardwood floors. Wagon-wheel fixtures hung from the cathedral ceiling, illuminating the staircase that rose to the next floor.

"This part of the ranch is off-limits to the family, so you don't have to worry about your privacy," he explained, ushering her through a doorway to the left wing where several rooms connected. The dogs were told to remain in the hall. "This used to be my study. There's a TV, and a stereo if you want to listen to music. Through there is the bathroom, and here's the bedroom."

Even before he turned on the lights, she could see reflections of firelight from the hearth flickering on the paneled walls. The room was a man's room, very rustic and simply furnished in curtains and bedspread of wide, jewel-toned stripes of claret, gold and green.

She felt slightly light-headed at the thought of sleeping in his king-size bed and could imagine how much Lucy would probably hate having to make a welcoming fire for Kit, in his bedroom no less.

"*Jarod*?"

Kit heard Lucy's voice call out and she turned to him. But the sudden shuttered look that robbed his face of its natural vitality prevented her from saying anything. They'd spent enough time together that she'd come to know the various expressions revealing his mood. Right now, she could feel a strange tension emanating from him.

"Wait here a moment." He put her overnight bag on the bed, then vanished the same way they'd come in.

"Thank heaven you're home." Lucy's voice carried to the bedroom. "I've been over at the bunkhouse waiting to intercept you. There's some lasagna in the oven for you and I've changed the sheets so you can sleep here tonight. The children are staying over at the Bradshaws' so that we can have some private time together."

Kit felt the blood drain from her face and stood there wishing the house would fall on top of her.

"I'm not alone," Jarod said in a dangerously soft voice. "Not an hour ago, I told you I'd see you and the children in the morning."

"I don't understand."

"I didn't ask you to," he clipped.

"Who's with you?"

"My receptionist from the clinic."

In the next breath, a frowning Jarod appeared in the bedroom doorway with Lucy right behind him.

"Linda, it seems my sister-in-law wanted to surprise me by preparing a meal."

Jarod was obviously in a dilemma, but no more so than Kit, who was having a difficult time recovering from the shock. In trying to keep Kit's identity a secret, he was forced to be abrupt with his sister-in-law.

The fact that the children were sleeping away for the night and that she'd laid a fire in his old bedroom meant this kind of thing had happened before. The pain of this latest revelation staggered Kit.

His sister-in-law looked almost ethereal in a knee-length dress of champagne-colored silk jersey that matched her shimmering blond hair. She was exquisite. *She was in love with Jarod.*

Because of Kit, Jarod couldn't respond the way he would have done if they'd been alone.

"Good evening, Mrs. Banning," Kit said in as cordial a voice as she could manage. After Lucy nodded, Kit went immediately to the fireplace to warm her hands, trying to avoid the other woman's scrutiny.

Earlier, Kit had removed her glasses and set them on the dresser. Now she wished she hadn't taken them off because she felt naked and exposed without them.

"The fire is welcome after the cold outside," she remarked for want of something, anything, to say to make things less awkward.

"Linda will be staying in my room while we're in Heber, Lucy. I'm glad you've already laid a fire. It's saved me the trouble. Linda..."

At the sound of her name on his lips, Kit turned in his direction, but refused to meet his level gaze.

"Since Lucy hasn't gone to bed yet, there are some matters we need to discuss. If you're hungry, go through the foyer to the kitchen at the rear and help yourself to anything you'd like. I'll join you there in a little while."

No. It would be much longer than a little while.

Placating his sister-in-law would take time, and Kit could picture the exact method he'd use to accomplish his objective. Images of his hands in Lucy's gilt hair, his mouth claiming her lips, devastated Kit.

"Don't worry about me, Dr. Banning. That hamburger filled me up and now I'm tired. I know how much you love your family, and naturally you have ranch business to attend to. Let's say goodnight and I'll see you in the morning."

"You're sure?" he demanded in a voice that sounded less than pleased.

"Of course." To make her point, Kit followed them to the exit. "Good night. Thank you for making me so comfortable."

"Good night," they both said at the same time. Kit avoided Jarod's eyes as she shut the door behind him.

"I can't understand why you didn't say anything about your receptionist accompanying you when we spoke on the phone earlier." Lucy's hurt voice carried from the corridor. But the outer door closed before Kit could hear Jarod's reply.

She had the grace to feel sorry for Lucy Banning. Being able to work with Jarod at the clinic must have been a godsend after her husband died. And when the grieving ended, she found herself in love with her husband's brother. What could be more natural?

Kit took off her coat and threw it on one of the twin couches facing the stone fireplace. For the first time ever, she understood the devastating effects of jealousy, an emotion that was tearing her apart.

Her plans to be alone with Jarod had gone up in smoke and Kit knew a terrible envy because Lucy was loved by him and had a permanent place in his heart.

Kit sighed soulfully and pulled off the wig. She hated it. If she could wash her hair, it might make her feel more comfortable and give her something to do before she finally went to bed.

How had she lived all these years without Jarod?

When her own nightmare ended, *if* it ended, would she have the strength to walk away from Jarod and never look back?

Something told her she was a one-man woman. The thought of living out the rest of her days without him didn't bear thinking about.

CHAPTER SIX

KIT had just finished dressing in a blouse and skirt and was putting on her wig when she heard a rap on the door. *Maybe it was Lucy.* Quickly, she grabbed her glasses and pushed them on her nose.

"Linda? Are you awake?"

Jarod.

The bedside clock said seven forty-five. Since Kit hadn't slept all night, agonizing over where *he* had spent the night, she was surprised that he was up this early.

"Come in."

He opened the door but just stood in the entrance. A brooding look darkened his features as he surveyed her in one sweeping glance, not missing a detail. She wanted to believe he couldn't help staring at her, that he'd grown used to her company and liked what he saw.

But in the clear light of day, she knew better. His assessment was purely clinical. First and foremost, he was a doctor, though he hadn't dressed like one this morning.

Beneath his leather jacket, the black turtleneck, faded jeans and cowboy boots fitted his well-honed body only too well. Kit swallowed hard. She couldn't even say good-morning. Embarrassed to be caught studying him every bit as thoroughly, she glanced away.

"I'm glad you're up," he said without preamble, making Kit feel guiltier than ever because her precarious situation had forced changes in his household. "Dart is meeting you for breakfast at the Chuck Wagon in five minutes. Once you've been introduced, I'll leave you two to talk while I go over to the office and catch up on some paperwork. Later, we'll take that sleigh ride."

Kit had no intention of going anywhere with Jarod unless it was to help out at his office. But judging by his enigmatic mood, she felt it wise to say nothing until she'd had her meeting with Mr. Thueson.

"I'm ready now."

She plucked her coat from the couch and slipped into it, then followed Jarod through the left wing to the foyer. With his back toward her, she could feast her eyes on his broad shoulders and not worry that he was aware of her avid interest.

Fred and Zelda met them at the front door and accompanied them to the Land Rover. A cold front had brought another drop in the temperature. The clear, frigid air stung her nostrils and sharply outlined the snow-covered mountains that rose twelve thousand feet and more to the west of the Heber Valley.

Kit shivered as she climbed inside the car and pulled the door shut before he could help her. To her surprise, the interior felt warm, which meant he'd been up for a while.

With a grimace, he went around to the driver's side and started up the engine. As they pulled away, they must have both seen Lucy at the same time. Her blond hair stood out as she hovered in the doorway.

Kit eyed him anxiously. "Jarod—"

"Let's save it for the time being," he broke in abruptly, reading her mind with uncanny perception. "Right now we need to concentrate on your problem."

Chastened, Kit clutched her hands together. He was right. Lucy was none of Kit's business. All that mattered was that the sooner she knew the identity of the person stalking her, the sooner she'd be out of his life. Then he and Lucy could get on with theirs.

On the short drive to the café, she felt his gaze wander over her profile several times. "That disguise is one hundred percent foolproof, as good as your wounded swan persona."

"It's all thanks to you," she said, her voice shaking. "You don't know how grateful I am for everything you've done. I realize you've had to put your personal life on hold and—"

"We've had this conversation before, Kit," he reminded her not unforcefully. "I'm getting my money's worth, so let's not waste our time dwelling on nonessentials." A tension-filled silence reigned until they came in sight of the café. As Jarod pulled the Rover over to the curb, he said, "I couriered the tape to Dart on Tuesday and we were up most of last night discussing it."

Maybe he hadn't been with Lucy after all. Kit's relief was palpable and she had to fight not to reveal the raw state of her emotions.

"I can't tell you what to do, but I urge you to put your trust in Dart no matter what strategy he has planned."

"That sounds ominous."

"I'll let you be the judge of that after you've heard him out."

On that cryptic note, he levered himself from the car and came around to assist her. Conscious of his hand at the back of her waist to guide her, they entered the café where she'd eaten many times in her life on her way to the hot springs located a few miles away.

The jukebox was playing a seventies tune and the booths were already crowded with farmers and ranchers who knew Jarod on sight. Everyone wanted to talk to him, their eyes full of friendly speculation because Jarod hadn't removed his hand from her waist yet. It was a miracle that they finally made it to the back dining room.

To Kit, Dart Thueson looked like a Texas Ranger. He wore sunglasses, sported a mustache and tan and was as lean and rugged as whipcord. When he stood up to shake her hand, he and Jarod appeared to be the same height and were similarly dressed. At least twenty-five years older than Jarod with more gray hair than brown, he was still a very attractive man and amazingly fit.

Her surprise must have shown on her face because Jarod whispered near her ear, "Keep in mind that he's been married to the same woman for thirty-seven years and just became a grandpa for the fifth time.''

His breath on her hot cheek sent a delicious shiver through her body. To cover the havoc he'd created, she whispered back, ''I must admit I was expecting someone more like Inspector Clouseau.''

Jarod passed that along to Dart and both men laughed loudly enough to draw the attention of several diners. With a squeeze to the side of her waist, he murmured, ''When you're through here, walk over to my office.''

Nodding her assent, she slipped into the seat across from Dart, who clapped Jarod on the shoulder, then sat down.

It was ridiculous how acutely she'd felt his touch, how lonely she felt when Jarod strode off. Her jealousy was definitely out of control. Every waitress in the place was smiling at him, trying to delay him with their flirting. For the first time in her life, Kit understood the expression about wanting to ''scratch their eyes out''. Her feelings were that explosive, that primitive.

One of them came over to their table. Dart removed his sunglasses and focused keen brown eyes on her face. ''Ms. Smith, what will you have for breakfast?''

Kit had forgotten about food but discovered she was hungry. ''Pancakes and sausage. And a small orange juice, please,'' she added at the last second.

After Dart gave his order and the waitress had gone, he took a swallow of the coffee she'd poured, then put his cup down and smiled at her. "Jarod was right. No one on the planet would know who you are in that getup."

"Thanks to Dr. Banning," she said, moistening her lips nervously.

"They don't come better." Something in his voice told Kit he'd just paid Jarod the supreme compliment.

She could echo his words. In fact, she wanted to shout to everyone in hearing distance that she'd found the perfect man, the kind of man heroes were made of.

But on the heels of her thoughts came the image of Lucy Banning, who'd already staked her claim.... How could Kit forget that for an instant?

Angry with herself for dwelling on the impossible, she rallied enough to give Dart her attention. "I'm more grateful than you'll ever know for being willing to help me. Dr. Banning thinks the world of you and told me I could trust you completely."

"I'm committed to finding out who's been making your life a living hell and having them put away."

"My only worry at the moment is that my sister must be hysterical. Jarod explained the reason why you didn't want me to contact her and Ross, but it's been more than a week now, and I'm terribly anxious about her."

"Naturally. But it would be better if we let another week go by before you talk to her."

Kit made a sound of protest.

"I know it's hard on you. But your vanishing act has made it possible for me to investigate the situation while the stalker has no inkling where to find you.

"Think about it. Once you speak to your sister, her relief will be immediately apparent and she'll give the game away. She won't be able to help herself. Even if she could keep a confidence of this magnitude, she'd be inclined to tell her husband."

"And he's a suspect," Kit murmured. She didn't want to admit that Dart's reasoning made perfect sense.

"Yes. But there's much more to it than that. Once it gets out that you're alive and safe, even if no one knows where you're hiding, this deranged person's behavior will undergo a change. That's what I'm looking for. That's why I need time to study the suspects at close range without anyone being aware of my covert surveillance.

"Only three people know where you are and who you are. You, Jarod and yours truly. Officially, your case is being handled by the police and the FBI. I have nothing to do with them. But because I'm still licensed to work on private investigations, I can nose around without anyone becoming suspicious. It puts me in a perfect situation. But I need more time."

"I can see that. And you're right. Laura doesn't hide her feelings. She'd never be able to keep this to herself."

"Exactly. No one could. Our loved ones are the most vulnerable at a time like this. But think of it this way. You're the one being pursued, not your sister. She has a husband and friends to rally around her. No matter her anguish, she's not the one being terrorized.''

When he put it like that, Kit didn't feel quite as guilty.

"This case won't take long to solve. Because of that tape, I've gleaned a good amount of information already. Combined with Jarod's insight and other conversations he's told me about, we'll be able to wind things up soon."

"You mean that?" she cried out anxiously.

"I wouldn't say it otherwise. Continue to wear your disguise. Stay away from TV and newspapers.''

"I'd like to be able to pay you a retainer but—"

"We'll worry about that when your stalker's caught," he interjected on a friendly note. "What I need is the list of names you made after your session with Jarod the other night."

"Yes. Of course." Kit reached for her purse and found the piece of paper with her notations. "Here." She handed it to him. "I hope it will help."

"It all helps," he remarked as the waitress brought their food to the table.

For the next fifteen minutes, she supplied him with a sketch of each person on the list while they ate. He asked more questions that prompted her to give the names of the few boys she'd dated in high school. He wasn't ruling anyone out.

"Jarod says you're a strong woman. It shows." He put the paper in his pocket and sat back. "We'll catch whoever it is. Each psychopath operates on his or her own peculiar, convoluted system. The trick is to tap into it and read the pattern correctly. Jarod's help will make the job easier because he understands human psychology so well. Once we're certain of the culprit's identity, then we'll lay the trap.''

Kit froze. "What kind?"

"It's quite simple. You'll go back to your old life and your stalker will come out of the woodwork again. One wrong move and we've got him.''

Kit shivered. The mere idea of going back to Stragi-Corp, of staying in her condo alone, filled her with dread. She felt that old stab of fear she'd been free of for the past week.

"We'll be with you every step of the way, Ms. Smith.'' He smiled kindly, conveying with much more than words his promise to stand by her. He stood up, pulled on a well-worn Stetson and left a couple of bills on the table. Tipping the rim of his hat, he said, "Have a good day. I'll ring Jarod tomorrow after I've had a chance to do some more investigating. Now you can finish your breakfast in peace.''

Kit thanked him profusely and said goodbye, but their conversation had robbed her of an appetite. After getting up from the table, she slipped into her coat and headed out of the café, too filled with adrenaline to stay seated.

Everything inside her rebelled at the thought of going back to her old life, not only for what she'd have to face, but for fear of losing Jarod. So deep was her turmoil, she forgot to look where she was going. If the driver of a semitrailer barreling through the main street of town hadn't honked his horn loudly enough to wake the dead, she would have been mowed down.

Kit didn't make it across the street any too soon and deserved the accusing stares coming her way as she hurried toward Jarod's office in the next block. No doubt, people thought of her as an empty-headed blonde, which was an unfair criticism of blondes in general. But since wearing the wig, she'd noticed a difference in the way she was treated.

Dr. Jarod Banning—Internal Medicine
Dr. Grayson Banning—Psychiatry

When she saw their names on the glass door, she felt a pang in her heart for Jarod because he'd so recently lost his brother. His life had had many losses. A wife, parents, his only sibling...

Thank God Kit still had Laura!

That was probably how Jarod felt about his sister-in-law and children. The sooner Kit got out of his life, the happier he and Lucy were going to be.

Kit prayed Dart was right—that it was only a matter of days or weeks before her case was solved. When Jarod had been so wonderful to her, the last thing she wanted to do was create more pain for him no matter how much her own heart was breaking.

"Jarod?" she called in a tremulous voice from the front reception area.

"Lock the door, then bring me the key," his deep voice responded. "I'm in the back office."

She did as he asked, then hurried past the front desk and down the hall, barely noticing the pictures and examination rooms.

A montage of impressive credentials was framed and hung behind the large walnut desk where Jarod was doing his paperwork. Kit gave him the key, then took a seat opposite him. He dropped his pen, then lounged back in the swivel chair.

"Can we talk?" she asked a trifle breathlessly, not knowing where to look because his striking features constantly drew her gaze.

"I've been waiting for you to finish up with Dart so we could do just that," he said in a quiet tone. His shrewd blue eyes fastened on her.

"I—I lay awake most of the night thinking about everything."

"That makes two of us," he returned, his regard never wavering. "At least for what was left of it."

Perhaps he hadn't joined Lucy after all. Kit was filled with a joy she had no right to feel.

Her knuckles stood out white as she gripped the arms of the chair tightly. "Would Lucy be out of a job if that taxi driver hadn't brought me to you?" she asked, her voice throbbing. "I want an honest answer."

"If you'll take off your glasses, I'll tell you the truth. We have the rest of the day to ourselves."

Kit ignored his request, disliking his patronizing attitude because it masked his real feelings.

"Look," she cried out, getting to her feet, "if you fabricated a job for me, then it can't help but have strained your relationship with Mrs. Banning. I—I felt sorry for her last night. If I'd been in her place, I wouldn't have understood your bringing a stranger into the house. This situation isn't her fault. It's mine!"

"Why do you always take the blame in any given situation? And for heaven's sake, sit down."

"Why?"

He sucked in his breath. "Because I feel at a disadvantage."

"That's absurd. You've never been intimidated by anything or anyone in your life."

"Maybe it's the wig." He scowled.

Her proud chin came up. "You chose it."

"I think we're having our first fight."

A long sigh escaped Kit and she sat down, removing her glasses. "I don't want to quarrel with you, Jarod." Her gray-green eyes softened. "You've been incredible. Don't you see? I don't want to complicate your life any more than I already have." Her voice choked up. "I owe you my life."

His jaw clenched. "There's that dreaded word, 'owe'. The one word I don't want to hear coming out of you, Kit. You had a choice, remember? Life, or maybe something else approaching death."

"And a wonderful job offer from you, with every amenity provided, including a bona fide doctor to help me work out my fears. Your worst trait is not accepting well-deserved praise graciously."

"Touché." His brow furrowed. "It's not every day a case like yours comes along. I couldn't resist," he admitted.

"Will you answer my original question?" she pleaded with him. "Helping me is one thing. Forcing Lucy to give up a job that has meant everything to her is another."

Jarod folded his arms. "You're right. The truth is, if you hadn't darkened my doorstep, she might have remained a part-time helper in this office for another three weeks, no longer. I need someone full-time with a medical background and word-processing skills. Lucy has neither of those qualifications. Hiring you constituted a stroke of genius on my part, forcing my hand sooner than I'd intended. But it achieved gratifying results."

Her eyes clouded. "How can you say that? I witnessed her devastation last night."

"What you saw and heard was a woman having to come face-to-face with her fears like the rest of us."

Kit blinked. "What fears?" With a man like Jarod to love her, Kit couldn't imagine Lucy wanting for anything.

"Letting go of past memories, for one. Growing old, for another. Proving herself in a faster-paced world, to name a third. Shall I continue?"

Confused, Kit asked, "Why does she have to prove herself?"

"Because she has lost her identity. It sometimes happens in marriage. She needs to take up her former career and earn a living again."

"I would have assumed your brother left her well-off. You said she owns the ranch."

"I'm talking about Lucy getting in touch with herself. She's a top-notch real-estate agent. My brother met her during the course of her work. She's the one who found this office for us.

"After they married, she gave it up to make a home and raise a family. It's time she stopped grieving and made an effort to heal. Until she's happy within herself, she won't be able to give happiness to anyone else, certainly not another marriage partner.

"The way she is right now, a man would feel he's a substitute for Grayson—an intolerable situation. Is that enough truth for you?"

Kit stared wide-eyed at Jarod. "Does she see you as another version of Grayson?"

He nodded with a solemn expression. "She still hasn't accepted his death. There's a strong family resemblance. He was three years my senior. As a family, we've been close."

She clenched her hands. "Human beings are so complicated." *Especially you, Jarod Banning. You want Lucy to come to you for yourself.*

He studied her pensive face through veiled eyes. "Do you still regard me as a monster?"

"I never thought that," she whispered in a hollow tone, "but I feel better knowing the truth." She bit her lower lip. "Does Lucy think you and I have something going on outside of work?"

He sat forward and put his arms on top of the desk. "You're a beautiful young woman, Kit. No doubt she noticed that the first time she saw you. Now others at the café have seen you with me. Within a few days, gossip will reach the local citizenry that my gorgeous blond receptionist lives with me." He grinned.

Kit couldn't see the humor. He might want to make Lucy jealous, but he'd pay a price. "It will hurt Lucy."

"On the contrary. It should make her sit up and take notice that I'm a flesh-and-blood human being with needs of my own. Not an extension of Grayson.

"What's nice about this arrangement is that Dart will have you at his beck and call any time of the day or night. I'd say it's a perfect solution all the way around. Best of all, my wounded swan, your reputation won't suffer."

"W-what do you mean?"

Their eyes linked.

"Because, you see, you don't really exist."

What should have been hilariously funny struck another deathblow to her heart. She'd be wise to remember that for Dr. Banning, she was just an interesting case he wanted to pursue. Nothing more....

"Kit," he grated.

"Yes?"

"Are you aware that when your emotions come too close to the surface, you fold up into yourself?"

She swallowed hard. He saw everything. "Did you know that when you want to be evasive, you answer a question with a question?"

"That's my business." He smiled wryly. "You know, you're not as tractable as I'd thought. Do you take after your mother or your father?"

"My mother, definitely."

"She kept your father happy?"

"She did, even through her sickness. Daddy said it was because she had a sixth sense. When I was little, I thought he was talking about her musical talent. When I grew up, I realized he meant that she had sex appeal."

Jarod's head went back and his deep laughter coincided with the sound of the telephone.

His response was automatic. By the third ring, he had the receiver to his ear. Suddenly, his smile vanished. An emergency must have cropped up.

"I'm afraid our sleigh ride will have to wait until later," he said after hanging up the phone. "That was the local hospital. Someone in a snowmobile accident with internal injuries. You can run me by the hospital, then keep the Rover and do whatever you want. I'll call you on the cellular phone when I'm ready to be picked up."

Kit should have been relieved rather than shattered that his plans for them had to be postponed.

Now that she knew the truth, she realized that if Jarod wanted to go for a sleigh ride, it was because he loved the outdoors, *not* because he wanted to be alone with her.

CHAPTER SEVEN

WITH the money Jarod gave her when she dropped him off at the hospital, Kit drove to the supermarket to pick up some toiletries and a few new books.

On her way inside the store, she received an unpleasant shock when she saw a handbill with a picture of herself tacked to the bulletin board along with several other flyers of missing children, dogs and cats.

The handbill read, "If you recognize this woman or have any information about her, please call the Salt Lake City Police Department," and it gave the local number.

Swamped by feelings of guilt, she hurried to pick up the things she needed, then got in the Rover and took off. For the next half hour, she drove aimlessly around the valley, her mind on Laura and Ross, who must be absolutely frantic by now.

It was one thing to eat breakfast and rationally discuss her disappearance with Dart, and quite another to come face-to-face with her own picture, knowing that Laura had worked with the police to get the handbills distributed.

While Kit was parked for a minute to watch the steam from the hot mineral spring form fascinating white plumes in the freezing air, the urge to call

Laura and let her know she was all right was over-powering. Despite Dart's reasoning, Kit couldn't bear to hurt her sister this badly when it wasn't necessary.

On impulse, she reached in the glove compartment for Jarod's cellular phone. While she sat there clutching it, debating whether to punch in the numbers or not, the phone rang. The sound gave her a jolt and the phone slipped from her hand to the floor. She grabbed for it and said hello.

"Kit?" It was Jarod. "Are you all right? You sound upset."

"Do I?" she responded nervously.

"Where are you?"

"Out by the hot pots."

"Why do I have this feeling something's wrong? Did Dart's plan upset you?"

It was on the tip of her tongue to tell him the truth, that she wanted to put Laura out of her misery. He wouldn't get mad at Kit, of course, but she knew he'd be disappointed if she wasn't able to follow Dart's advice.

From the beginning, Jarod had done everything in his power to help her, to make her feel safe. How could she let him down now? It wouldn't be fair to him, not when he'd placed himself in the position where the police could accuse him of withholding evidence and interfering with the law.

"I'm a little anxious," she confessed quietly.

"Kit—I know the thought of having to face your stalker when you go back to work is terrifying you. But Dart and I will be there. You won't be alone."

"I know," she replied, her voice trembling. "A-actually, if I sounded odd just now, it's because the phone fell on the floor and I was afraid you'd hang up before I could get it. Do you want me to come?"

After a lengthy pause while he weighed the sincerity of her words, he said, "I wish I could say yes, but another emergency has cropped up. It might be a couple of hours before I'm free. I'll call you as soon as I'm through. In the meantime, go back to the ranch and indulge yourself."

I'd rather indulge myself with you, Jarod Banning, her heart cried out.

She cleared her throat. "I bought some books and will take your advice."

"Don't get too engrossed. I'm planning on that sleigh ride." Then there was a click.

A voluptuous shiver ran through Kit's body. Ever since he'd mentioned it, she had imagined herself curled up in his strong arms beneath a blanket while their sleigh carried them through the silent snow.

The feelings aroused by that mental picture sustained Kit all the way back to the ranch. But her euphoria vanished when she discovered Lucy waiting for her inside the foyer, surrounded by the dogs.

Jarod's sister-in-law would look lovely in anything, but the silk blouse and tailored pants with suede vest was a particularly becoming outfit. Kit could see the disappointment in her eyes because Jarod hadn't come back with her.

Kit greeted her first, hoping to dispel some of the tension. "That's a beautiful outfit you're wearing."

"Thank you, Linda. I assume Jarod had an emergency of some kind?"

"Yes. He said he'd be at the hospital for a couple of hours."

It didn't matter how Kit responded. She could tell that no explanation would pacify Lucy. Since Kit didn't know if Jarod had told his sister-in-law that Kit would be taking over at the office, she didn't dare say anything. Worse, she knew the mention of a sleigh ride would hurt Lucy in ways Kit didn't even want to think about.

Since Jarod had shared a certain amount of information about Lucy, Kit felt more compassion for her and could tell she was living on her nerves.

"Have your children come home yet?"

"I'm expecting them any minute. Why?"

Improvising fast, Kit said, "I thought it might be fun to make a snowman with them. I never had any little brothers or sisters to play with."

Apparently, Kit's response was unexpected because Lucy warmed enough to say, "They'd probably love it."

"They're awfully cute children. You're very lucky. Tell them to come to my room when they want to play. I'll just be reading."

As Kit turned to go, Lucy asked a question that froze her in place. "Why did Jarod bring you to Heber?"

How was Kit supposed to answer that?

"Since I've been hired to work for him in Salt Lake, he thought it would be a good idea if I familiarized myself with the files at his office here. As I understand it, some of his patients will be driving to Salt Lake for their appointments now."

"That's odd. Since I'm the one helping with his patient load here, I'm surprised he didn't ask me to assist you."

"With your responsibilities as a mother, I think he wanted to spare you some of the work while he makes the move to the city."

Lucy still couldn't let it go. "How did you get the job? Were you a patient of his, or one of his colleagues?"

Alarmed, Kit didn't know how to respond. She could feel the perspiration break out on her forehead.

"I only asked because I can tell you're wearing a wig. Have you been in chemother—"

"Mommy!" Jennifer shouted, interrupting them. A heaven-sent blessing under the circumstances because it prevented Kit from having to answer. "Chet hit me with a snowball!"

"I didn't mean to." Chet brought up the rear, squeezing through the door at the same time as the dogs.

Both children ran over to hug their mother, then noticed Kit.

"Did you come with Uncle Jarod?" Chet wanted to know.

"Yes."

Jennifer stared at Kit for an uncomfortably long moment. "Are you his girlfriend?"

"Of course not," Lucy said in a disgusted voice. "She's helping out your uncle at the office."

"Where is he?"

Chet's question had been directed at Kit, but Lucy answered. "At the hospital. You can see him later. Did you two eat breakfast?" They both nodded. "Then get yourselves bundled up and Linda will help you build a snowman."

"Cool." Chet grinned.

"Are you going to come outside too, Mommy?"

"Not today."

Kit saw the disappointment on the children's faces and turned to Lucy. "Do you have a pair of gloves I could borrow?"

"Of course. We keep lots of spares in the laundry room behind the kitchen. Chet can get them for you. Did you bring boots?"

"No."

"Jennifer?" She turned to her daughter. "Run up to Mommy's closet and bring down my old galoshes for Linda. They ought to be big enough to fit her."

"Okay. I'll be right back. Don't start without me."

"Tell you what," Kit said. "I'll meet you both out front in five minutes. That will give me enough time to put my things away and freshen up."

After a shout of glee, both children ran off. Kit thought she could escape, too, but she was wrong. Lucy followed her through to Jarod's bedroom.

"Linda—forgive me for being so personal, but if you've been ill, maybe you shouldn't go outside. Sometimes the children get too excited and unruly."

Kit had difficulty keeping up with Lucy. One minute, she behaved like a woman whose territory was being threatened. The next, she sounded totally sincere. No matter, Kit needed to set her straight about the state of her health.

"I'm not sick, Mrs. Banning. I needed a job and responded to Dr. Banning's ad for a receptionist."

"He *did* run an ad, then," Lucy said in a haunted whisper. Kit felt terrible about it, but there was nothing else to do. The truth had to come out.

"As for this wig," Kit continued, "I'm wearing it to cover up the terrible haircut the beautician gave me last week. You know how it is when you ask them to take off a few inches and they lop off ten. It's so short right now, I'm embarrassed for anyone to see me the way it is. In another week or so, it'll be grown out enough that I won't need the wig. If you've never worn one, you have no idea how hot and uncomfortable it is. I hate it," Kit blurted out in total honesty.

"Can you run a computer, do word processing?"

This was getting worse. The woman was so upset about losing her place in Jarod's life, she scarely heard Kit's explanation about the wig.

"Yes." Kit busied herself putting the things from the sack on her dresser. "I had to learn it for my last job."

"What kind of work did you do?"

"Hey, Linda?" The children came dashing into the bedroom. "We thought you'd be outside!"

"Your mother and I were talking, but I'll be there in a minute."

Jennifer thrust the galoshes at her. "Here. Try them on."

"I found you some gloves." Chet held them up. "Great."

Thankful that the children had interrupted them, Kit tugged on the boots, slipped her hands into the well-worn gloves and ushered the children out of the room.

She felt Lucy's gaze as the three of them ran through the snow with the dogs in close pursuit. Chet had already decided the snowman would be built next to the pine trees.

After a few minutes, Lucy shut the door. The children must have noticed because Jennifer said, "I bet she's crying again."

"Yeah." This from Chet.

"One day she'll stop," Kit murmured as she helped them roll the huge ball that would form the base.

"That's what Uncle Jarod said."

"Well, your uncle is right."

"I wish he didn't have to move to Salt Lake."

"He'll always come back for visits, Chet. Think how much fun that will be!"

"I wish Daddy didn't have to die."

Kit eyed Jennifer tenderly. "I know how you feel."

Both children stared wide-eyed at her. "You do?"

"My Daddy died about a year before yours."

Jennifer's chin wobbled. "Did you cry a lot?"

"Yes," Kit answered honestly. "Probably because my mother died before he did."

"You don't have a mommy anymore?" Jennifer cried out.

Kit gave the little girl a squeeze. "No. So just think how lucky you are to have such a beautiful mommy. Right now she's sad because she loved your daddy a lot, but in time, she'll start to laugh again."

"Do you laugh a lot?"

Out of the mouths of babes.

"I'm working on it, Jennifer."

Together, they rolled up the second ball, which would form the trunk, and struggled to shove it on top of the first.

"That's what Uncle Jarod always says. I'm working on it, Chet."

"Well, let's see if we can get this snowman built before he comes home. Once we have the head formed, how shall we dress him?"

"I'll run in the house and get some of Dad's old stuff."

"Good idea, Chet," Kit encouraged him. "Why don't you do that now while Jennifer and I finish rolling up this last ball?"

Jennifer put her hands on her hips. "Why do we always have to make it a man? Why can't it be a queen?"

"*A queen?*" Chet derided.

Kit chuckled. Jennifer was a woman after her own heart. "Why not?"

"Okay," he conceded. "But let's make her real ugly."

"No! She's going to be beautiful. I have some pretty things to dress her in. I'll get them right now."

"And I'll get some hay from the barn for her hair."

"She doesn't need hair."

"Whoever heard of a bald queen?"

"The one in *Snow White*. You'll see."

Jennifer took off like a shot and almost ran into her mother, who was hurrying out to the Land Rover. When the little girl disappeared inside the house, Lucy waved to Kit and Chet.

"Jarod phoned. I'm going to pick him up and get a few groceries. We'll be home soon."

Kit knew exactly how Chet felt. Before he could protest that he wanted to go, too, she called out, "That's fine, Mrs. Banning. I'll watch the children for you."

Lucy conveyed her thanks from the car window and drove off.

Kit hurriedly turned to Chet and winked at him. "Let's finish this in time to surprise your uncle."

"Yeah."

"Why don't you find a big stick we can use for the queen's scepter?"

Giving him an important job was the right thing to do. He forgot to be unhappy and headed toward some fruit trees at the side of the house.

No sooner had he gone than Jennifer came tripping out the door carrying a mysterious treasure in her arms. Kit could hardly wait to see what she'd drummed up.

But her curiosity changed to horror when she saw a long slash of purple color trailing through the snow.

The satin cape!

As Jennifer ran toward her carrying the swan costume and headdress, Kit could feel the blood drain from her face. Moistening her lips, which had gone as dry as parchment, she said, "W-where did you find these things?"

"In one of the drawers at Uncle Jarod's new house."

Aghast, Kit whispered, "Did he tell you you could have them?"

"Yes. The people who moved out left a lot of stuff. He said I could take whatever I found upstairs as long as it wasn't his. Will you put this on her head?"

She thrust the feather headdress at Kit, who could hardly believe her eyes.

Never in her wildest dreams could she have conceived of this kind of complication. If she tried to thwart Jennifer, she was afraid the little girl would make a scene that might provoke questions—the *last* thing Kit wanted to have happen.

With trembling hands, she took the headdress and fitted it over the top ball, praying as she'd never prayed before that Lucy would be too distracted and preoccupied to care about the snowman or question where the items had come from.

"Here's a mouth from my Minnie Mouse Halloween costume to put on her, and here's some black checkers for her eyes."

The grotesque smiling lips and white teeth looked amazingly real on the snow queen coming to life before them.

"You put in the eyes."

Kit lifted Jennifer from the ground and let the little girl finish her creation.

"Now you have to throw the feathers around her neck."

Every part of her shaking, Kit took the costume that had adorned her own body the night she'd fled the ballet in terror, and draped it around the seam between the two balls. The queen was starting to take on a definite persona.

Jennifer scrambled for the cape and handed it to Kit. Wordlessly, she grasped the satin material in her hands and fastened it around the neck. The flowing purple material almost completely covered the trunk and base, adding the final, single most important touch.

Dear God. Kit could just imagine Jarod's shock when he saw it. As for Lucy's reaction, Kit was beginning to get scared.

"Hey—that's cool!" Chet enthused, running up to them with a three-foot stick. "She looks like Mirror Mirror On The Wall!"

She did. The police would have no trouble identifying Kit's getaway outfit if they saw it.

"I told you she didn't need hair!"

Jennifer was right. Not only was Lucy's daughter smart, she had more imagination than any little girl Kit had ever known.

Helpless at this point, she watched in silence as the children chatted feverishly, anticipating the grown-ups' reaction.

It was left to Chet to poke the stick in the waist so it protruded from the material. From a distance, it would look exactly like a scepter.

Wringing her hands, Kit questioned over and over again why Jarod hadn't gotten rid of the costume. But the more she agonized, the more she realized that he probably hadn't thrown it out for fear someone would find it and trace it to his house. Aside from burning the outfit, he probably felt it was safest hidden away in one of his upstairs drawers.

It brought to mind something her father once told her. That children were ingenious. Put them behind enemy lines and they'd create total chaos. *How true those words.*

"Here they come!" Chet cried out and started running toward the Land Rover. Jennifer followed closely behind, thrilled with their masterpiece and eager to show it off.

Kit trailed at a distance, waiting....

"Come and see our snowman!" Jennifer shouted to Jarod, grabbing his hand once he'd alighted from the car. Kit's heart leaped to her throat the moment she saw him.

"Come on, Mom," Chet urged. "It's real rad."

To Kit's chagrin, Lucy obeyed her son and the four of them, plus the dogs, approached the amazing snow figure.

Kit couldn't watch and closed her eyes.

"Well, well. What have we here?" Jarod murmured, sounding exactly as he did the night he removed the edges of the cape from Kit's body. "The wicked queen, in Mrs. Baxter's old castoffs, no less."

Upon that remark, Kit's eyes flew open to meet the enigmatic gleam in Jarod's. As far as she was concerned, he deserved some kind of medal. In an instant, his razor-sharp brain had comprehended everything. He'd covered his ground so well, his sister-in-law would never be the wiser.

"It's remarkable, Linda," Lucy half gasped.

"The credit goes to your daughter, Mrs. Banning." She practically croaked getting the words out and tore her gaze from Jarod's. "This was her creation from beginning to end. Except for the scepter, which was Chet's contribution."

"Yeah. I wanted a snowman but Jennifer said we had to make a queen. It's pretty good for a girl," he conceded.

"Can we take a picture, Uncle Jarod?"

"I was thinking the same thing, Jenny," he murmured in a pensive tone, but only Kit knew the reason for it. "Chet, run and get my camera out of the cupboard in the study, will you, son?"

"Sure, Uncle Jarod!"

"Come up here." Jarod reached down and lifted Jenny in his arms. Slowly, he circled the queen, inspecting everything his niece pointed out to him. "I think you've outdone yourself this time." He kissed the end of her freckled nose, winning Jenny's undying devotion.

Jarod had such a remarkable rapport with people, with children, it was no wonder his family adored him. Kit couldn't blame Lucy for wanting to hold on to him. After losing her husband, it would be too painful to let Jarod go, too. He would be an impossible man to replace.

Kit was beginning to realize that it had been a mistake to come to the ranch. Not only because of the threat of exposure, but because she felt like an intruder in their private lives. There were complicated, deep-seated issues here that had nothing to do with her.

"Come on, Linda. Get in the picture!" Chet urged and pulled her after him. Shocked to see that he'd returned and she hadn't even noticed, Kit did his bidding while Jarod took several poses.

When they were finished, Kit walked over to Jarod and took the camera from him. Studiously avoiding his gaze, she said, "Let me get one of you with your family."

She raised the camera to eye level and focused in on the Bannings. Through the lens, Kit could stare at Jarod, whose provocative masculine features and build were almost too attractive. It wasn't fair. The four of them looked like they belonged together. Her heart shattered into a thousand pieces.

After taking three poses she said, "I think that must be the end of the film."

Chet ran over to see and Kit told him to give the camera back to his uncle.

"If you'll all excuse me, I need to go in the house." Not waiting for anyone's approval, she took off through the snow as fast as the galoshes would allow.

Thankful to reach the privacy of her living quarters, Kit sank onto the bed emotionally exhausted and started to remove her gloves and boots.

"Kit?"

She raised her head in time to see Jarod slip inside the room and shut the door.

"Don't take off your coat. We're leaving."

"We can't," she said without hesitation. "The children have been waiting for you. They'll be crushed if we go on a sleigh ride without them." *Lucy will be crushed.*

"There's been a change in plans." His mouth hardened. "We'll talk about it in the car. Let's go."

At this moment, he was unapproachable and Kit knew better than to argue. In truth, she had no right to question his decisions, not when she'd willingly submitted to his plans to help her.

Reaching for her purse, she followed him from the room and out of the house to the Rover. There was no sign of Lucy, thank heaven, but the second the children saw them, they made a beeline for the car with the dogs leading the way.

"Where are you going, Uncle Jarod?"

"I brought Linda along to help me at the office, Chet."

"Can we come?"

"Not this time. Why don't you two make a king to go with that queen while we're gone?"

"Chet can," Jenny grumbled.

"In that case, I suggest you go inside and help your mother fix dinner. See you later, guys."

Chet said something else but Kit didn't catch it because they were moving. Once they'd cleared the ranch, she thought Jarod would explain what was going on, but the awful silence only deepened.

Within a couple of minutes, they were driving down the main street. When Jarod unexpectedly turned the car into a parking lot and pulled up next to a motel office, she darted him a questioning glance.

"Relax, Kit. I'm not about to seduce you."

Struck to the raw, she retorted, "I know that."

"Do you?" he grated before he levered himself from the car and disappeared into the lobby.

He was back before she'd had time to figure out what exactly he'd meant by that remark. Without saying a word to her, he drove them to a unit near the end, away from the street.

Nodding in the direction of the restaurant adjacent to the parking lot, he said, "I'll call for Chinese and they'll bring it over." Until he'd mentioned it, she hadn't realized how hungry she was. Jarod came around and helped her from the car, then ushered her inside the motel room. "You freshen up while I phone. Then we'll talk."

Alarmed by his ominous tone, Kit was thankful for the respite. After removing her coat, she closeted herself in the bathroom to remove the glasses and wig. It was heaven to be able to look in the mirror and recognize the person staring back.

She washed her face, then put on fresh lipstick and combed her hair. Finally, she was starting to feel a little bit like herself again.

When she came out of the bathroom, Jarod was standing at the end of the queen-size bed, his legs slightly apart. His gaze was solemn as he surveyed her for an overly long moment. Her face went hot from his perusal, which seemed incredibly intimate in the confines of the motel room.

"I knew Lucy wouldn't like having another woman in the house, but her jealousy of you is out of control," he began without preamble. "If I had known how thoroughly she would grill you while I was at the hospital, I would never have told you to go back to the ranch."

"It's all right," she murmured on a shallow breath. His nearness was swamping her with emotions she didn't know how to handle. "I just hope I said the right things."

"Your responses were perfect."

Running a hand through her black curls, she said, "I didn't know whether to make a fuss about the costume or not."

The corner of his mouth lifted a fraction. "Trust Jenny to have found it."

"I almost fainted when I saw her bring it outside."

"There's been no harm done. But under the circumstances, you'd better stay here until we return to Salt Lake."

"I—I agree that would be for the best," she said, rubbing her palms against her hips with unknowing provocation. Jarod seemed fascinated by the movement, making her more aware of him than ever. "For some reason, my presence is threatening. She's terrified I'm going to take over her job at the office."

"She's terrified of a great deal more than that," he declared in a husky voice.

The air was so charged with tension, Kit's mouth went dry and her legs felt heavy. When the knock came at the door, it was such a surprise she staggered for a moment and had to cling to the edge of the television stand.

The food. She'd forgotten all about his ordering it. In a kind of stupor, she watched him pay the delivery boy and set the sack of cartons on the table in the corner. But instead of inviting her to join him for a meal, he said something quite different.

"While you eat, I'll run back to the ranch and get the rest of your things."

The last thing she wanted was for him to leave. Lucy would probably find some way to detain him. Kit's disappointment was greater than she would have believed. That's when she realized she'd fallen hopelessly in love with him.

"I—I thought you wanted to talk."

After an interminable moment, he replied softly, "I thought so, too."

Devastated, she asked, "Why don't you at least stay long enough to eat while the food's hot? Aren't you hungry?"

By now his hand was on the doorknob. "Yes. But not for Chinese."

CHAPTER EIGHT

AN HOUR later, Kit picked herself up from the bed where she'd been sobbing.

Face it. He's not coming back until he has to.

Like an automaton, she plodded barefoot to the table and sat down to eat. She had no idea if the Chinese was good, only that it was food. If she didn't put something in her stomach soon, she knew she'd be sick.

In a few minutes, she'd eaten enough to ward off the hunger pains, then pushed the rest away, her swollen eyes staring into space.

Last night, Lucy had been waiting for Jarod to arrive from Salt Lake. But because of Kit, he'd had to follow another agenda.

But not tonight.

Tonight he'd wanted to be with Lucy and had taken the necessary steps to make certain Kit was out of the way. If part of Jarod's plan had been to make Lucy jealous—so she'd begin to see him for who he really was—then he'd succeeded admirably.

Kit had no right to be upset about any of it. From the beginning, Jarod had never pretended to be anything but the Good Samaritan. How could she complain about the way he lived his personal life when he was willing to keep her, Kit, safe and sane until the stalker was caught?

She couldn't! Not without being the most ungrateful wretch who ever breathed. All he'd asked was that Kit work as his assistant until she went back to her old life. He needed and deserved the best receptionist he could find. She wanted to be that person. It was the least she could do considering he had saved her life!

Falling in love with him was *her* problem, not his. She'd better learn to deal with it starting right now, but it hurt. Kit had never experienced a pain like it.

For want of anything better to do, she turned on the TV, then lay down on the bed still dressed in her skirt and blouse and half listened to a couple of sitcoms. She was just dozing off when ten o'clock rolled around. The local anchorman was giving news highlights when something he said had Kit sitting straight up on the bed.

"One week has gone by since the mysterious disappearance of Kit Mitchell, the young chemical engineer from Stragi-Corp, who was last seen at a performance of *Swan Lake*. The police are investigating a new lead. It appears a swan costume and cape also disappeared from the backstage dressing room of the theater Saturday night, although they can't prove a connection."

Kit gasped.

"Since there has been no ransom note, police are investigating the possibility that Ms. Mitchell may have been the victim of foul play. Sources indicate that before her disappearance, she had been receiving anonymous threats on her life. Informants close to the family are now concerned about the victim's sister who has been hospitalized since the unfortunate incident occurred. Police are still asking that anyone who—''

Hospitalized?

Kit flipped off the remote as a chill ran through her body. Without hesitation, she lunged for the phone directory on the bedside table. Hopefully, Dart Thueson's number was listed. She'd rather call him than disturb Jarod, but she'd do what she had to do.

If Laura was sick enough to be sent to the hospital over this, then Kit refused to be the cause of her sister's illness one second longer than necessary.

A cursory glance of the *T*s indicated that Dart's number was unlisted. Frustrated and shaky, she hunted for Jarod's number, which she knew would be there since he was a doctor.

That's when she heard a knock on the door. ''Kit?'' The low, masculine voice she would always respond to called out, ''Are you asleep?''

She flew off the bed and flung the door wide. ''Thank God you've come. Laura is in the hospital. I was just going to phone you,'' she cried as Jarod entered the room, carrying her overnight bag. To her shock, Dart walked in behind him.

The presence of both men dwarfed the tiny room and sent her over the edge. She put a hand to her mouth and closed her eyes, but tears fell freely down her ashen cheeks.

"Something terrible has happened to her. S-she's not—"

"No, Kit, she's not." Suddenly, she was caught close in Jarod's arms and he buried his hand in her curls while she sobbed her relief against his shoulder.

"The media exaggerates everything out of proportion, Ms. Mitchell," Dart interjected. "Two days ago, your sister was hospitalized in order to prevent another miscarriage. She's doing fine. I've just talked to her doctor."

"You're kidding!" Kit wiped her eyes and pulled away from Jarod, embarrassed to have broken down like that. "Laura's really pregnant again?"

Dart nodded. "That's right."

"Jarod!" She turned instinctively to the man she loved, wanting to share this one small happiness with him.

His mouth curved into an answering smile, but she didn't imagine the strange flicker that came and went in his eyes.

With a glance that included both of them, she said, "I guess you know the police have found out about the missing costume."

"That was common knowledge the night you ran off in it," Dart muttered. "Jarod tells me the incriminating evidence now adorns a certain queen for the whole world to see." He tried to hold back the laughter, but couldn't. Jarod joined him.

In and of itself, Jennifer's discovery of the costume and her ingenious idea was terribly funny. But too much was at stake for Kit to smile. Biting her lip, she said, "If Lucy watched the news tonight, then—"

"She's probably put two and two together by now," Jarod interjected, reading her mind.

Dart sat down in one of the chairs and leaned forward. "What Jenny did hasn't ruined anything. Only changed the timetable. We have plans to make. By Monday, you'll be back in Salt Lake and everyone will know about it."

"Monday...!" she gasped, searching his face anxiously. Debilitating fear sent icy tentacles over her body.

Jarod pulled her down on the bed next to him. "Another few days won't make that much difference. Dart's ready to set the trap."

She tortured the pleats of her skirt with trembling fingers. "Does this mean you have an idea who's been stalking me?"

"Yes. In fact, I'd stake all my years on the force that I know the identity of the culprit."

Adrenaline poured through her body in pulsating waves. "I'm terrified to ask my next question," she breathed shakily.

"I wouldn't answer it."

Her head flew back. "What do you mean?" Unable to help herself, she turned to Jarod for comfort.

He covered her hand and squeezed it gently. "Dart's trying to tell you that for the same reason your sister had to remain in the dark, now you will have take up your life once again as Kit Mitchell, without knowing the name of your pursuer."

"I can't!"

Dart didn't react. "It's the only way we'll catch the psychopath red-handed."

Kit started to shake uncontrollably and finally jumped up, pulling her hand away from Jarod. "I can't do it. I'll fall apart. You don't know what I went through before I ran way."

"That's right," Dart concurred. "We don't. Somehow you're going to have to find the courage and deal with this. You can do it."

Kit fought the tears as he spoke.

"At this point, I know more about yourself than you do. The dean of engineering at the university told me you were the department's choice for the best engineering student three years straight. That kind of success in a male-dominated field speaks of your intelligence and courage.

"The nurse who took care of your mother couldn't praise you enough for your strength at a time when many loved ones fall to pieces, unable to cope. According to her, you were the glue that held your family together."

With bowed head, Kit turned away from both of them, trying to come to terms with an untenable situation.

"I'm going to leave now. Talk it over with Jarod. If you can't bring yourself to go back on Monday, then you can't. But the sooner you bring this thing to an end, the sooner you can start living again. Right?''

A heavy sigh escaped her lips. She clenched and unclenched her hands, afraid she'd never be ready to face her fear.

From the open door he said, ''You can call your sister tonight.''

''I can?'' She spun around.

''I think it's time to put both of you out of your misery.''

''What will I say to her? I—I don't know if I can go back to Salt Lake on Monday.''

''Tell her you're safe, that you had to get away to gain some perspective, that you'll be home soon. Beyond that, discuss anything you like. Hearing from you will relieve any stress in that department.

''She has a private room at the hospital. The police have put a tracer on her phone. In anticipation of your call, I jotted down the number of the pay phone in the waiting room down the hall.

''She's allowed to use a wheelchair, I understand. So if she's called to the phone, I'm confident they'll let her take it. If not, her husband can come to the phone. He's been at her side almost continually.''

''I'm thankful to hear that,'' Kit moaned. ''But I thought you didn't want anyone to know about me until I went back.''

''The situation has changed. Let me know what you intend to do after you've talked to your sister. Jarod knows how to reach me.''

"All right," she said in a solemn voice. "Thank you for everything."

"I know this is hard. But remember the shape you were in when the taxi drove you to Jarod's clinic. Good night."

His parting words resounded in her head. Since meeting Jarod, her life had changed drastically. She didn't know herself anymore.

"Kit?" Jarod murmured. "I have to leave, too, but I'll be back in a little while. I need to talk to Lucy before she says or does something that could jeopardize your situation."

"That's fine," she lied. "I'd like to be alone right now."

He frowned. "You're sure?"

She nodded and opened the door for him. Kit understood exactly why Jarod was leaving. He needed to see Lucy and assure her that the agony was almost over, that Kit would be gone out of their lives on Monday.

"I won't be long."

"Don't worry about it, Dr. Banning."

With a reluctance she could feel, he strode away from her and took off in the Land Rover.

She wished she could do the same and decided she'd take a walk in the freezing night air to clear her head before she called Laura. Her sister wouldn't be satisfied with vague answers. Kit would have to be on her toes to protect Jarod and his family.

After putting on her coat, she reached for her purse and left the room at a brisk pace. High cloud cover blotted out the stars, but the main street was still lighted enough that she wasn't nervous walking around.

Strange to think of Jarod living here all these years and she hadn't known of his existence. How many times had she traveled to Heber for dinner and a swim at the hot pots? Would life ever be the same after knowing him? *Living with him*?

What other man would ever interest her after this? Jarod said he would never force her to do anything. He certainly wouldn't make her go back to Salt Lake on Monday if she couldn't handle it.

If only she could put off the decision indefinitely and stay with him where she felt protected and cherished.

As she walked block after block past the various storefronts, tears froze to her cheeks, but she was oblivious and kept reliving the week she'd spent at his clinic. It had been the happiest time of her life, falling in love....

When she reached the movie theater, she decided a Bruce Willis movie was exactly what she needed and went inside. Ten minutes later, she left, too distraught to concentrate.

Not until she reached the next intersection did she realize a car had been following her. It was the Land Rover!

"Get in," Jarod muttered in a stern voice, and opened the door on her side.

She did his bidding then closed it. "You sound angry. What's wrong?"

"Worried, concerned, anxious might begin to cover what I'm feeling," he snapped. "I've been at the motel waiting for you for the past twenty minutes. Did you speak to your sister? Is that why you went off without leaving word where you'd be?"

His concern thrilled her. "I—I won't apologize for my thoughtlessness since you hate it when I do."

"This is one time when you should."

"I'm sorry, Jarod. I thought a movie might help calm me down, but of course it didn't. To answer your question, I haven't called Laura yet because I'm still trying to figure out what to say."

"If you'd waited for me to come back, we could have brainstormed together."

"But I didn't know when that would be, did I? Generally, something comes up that keeps you longer than you'd intended. I certainly didn't mean to upset you."

"It's dangerous on this street at night, particularly for a beautiful woman who is out walking alone."

"You've made your point, Doctor."

He bit out an epithet and drove over the speed limit to reach the motel. In this mood, he was capable of anything. The minute he brought his Rover to a standstill, she opened the door and got out.

Jarod caught up to her as she put the key in the lock and went inside. He followed after and shut the door. They faced each other like adversaries.

"What prevented you from calling Laura as soon as Dart left?"

"I needed to think things through so I wouldn't endanger you or your family."

"I think there's more to it than that."

"What do you mean?"

"You're not sure of her response."

Kit looked away, unable to sustain his regard because he could always see through her. "That's true. As soon as I call her—" she paused, searching for the right words "—as soon as she knows I'm all right—"

"She'll make you feel guilty because you went off without telling her. All those old feelings of self-doubt will come back because you once heard her ask her husband if you had made up those notes to get attention."

Jarod's observations rendered her speechless.

"She'll probably accuse you of being selfish and thoughtless, only concerned with yourself."

"You even sound like her," Kit whispered incredulously.

"Tell me more about Laura. Your first memory of her."

Kit rubbed her arms. "There are so many of them."

"You're right. And often we have a tendency to remember the bad ones with more clarity," he murmured.

"How true." She gave a sad laugh. "Like the Christmas Mom and Dad gave us ukuleles. Daddy taught us a few tunes, and that night I can still remember how proud I felt because I could play 'Jingle Bells'.

"He praised me in front of Laura. She threw her instrument on the floor and ran out of the room saying Daddy loved me best. I remember chasing after her and telling her how sorry I was. That I knew Daddy loved her, too, and it didn't matter that she didn't like the ukulele."

"And you've been saying you're sorry ever since," Jarod inserted. "No doubt you've apologized repeatedly for your brilliant academic marks."

"It got to the point where I never showed her my grades or discussed my schoolwork with her," Kit confessed.

"Is it still a mystery why you're hesitant to talk to her? I think you've grown tired of having to say you're sorry one more time," he observed, driving his point home.

"Jarod—your insight into human nature absolutely astounds me."

"That's because I worked around my big brother long enough to learn something about the mind. It's so powerful, it determines the physical health of our bodies to a great extent."

Her eyes feasted on his masculine beauty. "What if I hadn't met you? I can't imagine where I'd be, what kind of shape I'd be in by now!"

He pursed his lips. "You'd have found help from another source, Kit."

Without conscious thought, she moved toward him and kissed his cheek, unbearably aware of his smooth-shaven jaw and the scent of his soap. "Thank you," she whispered, loving him more completely at this moment than ever before. "I'm ready to phone Laura."

"Good girl," he murmured thickly. "I'll let you speak to her in private."

"No, please..." Kit panicked. "I want you to stay, unless—"

"I'm only going next door, Kit."

"Next door?"

"Dart and I arranged it with the manager. From the front desk, he can work it so you and I can be on the phone at the same time when you call Laura. I'm not going to listen in, but I'll tape it. Later, in case you want to talk with me about any part of your conversation with her after you've hung up, you'll have a record of what was said."

Her eyes moistened once more. "Thank you."

Knowing Jarod would be next door released her from the fear that had gripped her earlier. In its place was a strange calm. For the first time in her life, she began to understand the accusation-apology syndrome of her relationship with Laura. Not in all its ramifications, but enough to give her an edge.... Only Jarod could have done this for her.

"Here's the number Dart wrote for you." Before she realized what was happening, he cupped her face in his hands and pressed a kiss to her forehead. "Good luck." Then he was gone.

*   *   *

"Hello? Who's calling? You've reached a pay phone," said a male voice.

"Is this Brighton Hospital?"

"Yes."

"Are you one of the orderlies?"

"No. My son is a patient."

"I see. Would you be kind enough to ask a nurse at the station nearby to come to the phone please?"

"Sure. Just a minute."

Kit could hear the hospital intercom and the sound of a cart rattling through the corridor.

"This is Stacey. Can I help you?"

"Yes. Would it be possible to speak to Laura Hunter?"

"Not right now. She's sleeping."

"Is her husband there? May I speak to him?"

"I'll have to check. Who's calling?"

"A relative. I only heard about Laura's condition a little while ago."

"Hold on."

A minute went by. Then, "This is Ross."

Kit took a deep breath. "Ross—it's Kit."

A shocked gasp came over the wire. "Kit? I don't believe it! Kit?" he cried out again. "Good Lord, where are you? How are you? Are you all right? Are—"

"I'm fine," she broke in. "Really fine. I had to go away for a time to think everything out. I'm perfectly safe, and I'll be coming home soon. I have to speak to Laura."

"You don't sound like yourself at all," he bit out. "Is there someone there with you? Kit—have they kidnapped you? Are they letting you talk to prove that you're still alive?''

"Calm down, Ross," she urged. "No one kidnapped me. The night of the ballet that psychopath left another calling card." She heard a harsh sound come out of his throat. "I tried to find you and Laura, but I couldn't. I was so frightened, I decided to run away."

A long silence ensued. "All this time I've thought of you at the mercy of some pervert. Why didn't you tell *me*, at least? I would have kept your secret. Do you have any conception of what this has done to me?"

Instead of feeling devastated, a sad smile broke out on Kit's face. Ross would always run true to form. Always think of himself first. "That's why I'm calling. To reassure you," she explained without emotion. "The nurse said Laura was sleeping. Shall I call back?"

"Hell, no! Don't hang up! If we lose this child, it will be your fault. I know you were terrified, Kit, but to run away and never say a word. I don't think Laura will ever forgive you."

Kit blinked. If he'd said that to her before she'd met Jarod, she would have gone to pieces.

"And you, Ross? Won't you forgive me, either?"

He exhaled a deep breath. "Hell, Kit. What a question. Where are you? Can I come and get you?"

"I'll come back when I'm ready, not before."

"You sound different. Are you in Salt Lake? At least tell me that much before I put Laura on the line."

Being away for a week gave Kit new insight. Maybe Ross was her stalker, but with Jarod standing behind her, she wasn't as frightened at the possibility. "That's not important. Will you get her for me?"

"What's happened to you?" he asked with genuine puzzlement.

"I've had time to think. In a life-and-death situation, one tends to evaluate one's past, Ross. The time apart has done me a world of good."

"At everyone else's expense," he mumbled under his breath. "Look, if you'd wanted to escape, Laura and I could have taken you someplace. Out of the country, even."

"You don't understand, Ross. I had to be on my own for a change."

He sucked in his breath. "What if you get another note after you come back? Will you run away again? None of us could handle it."

She tightened her grip on the receiver. "No more running, Ross. I intend to face whoever is out there."

"Your room's ready at the house. Laura wouldn't touch anything. She's prayed night and day for you to come back."

Kit had never known Laura to pray. Maybe she did. Prayer was an individual matter, but coming from Ross, she found his words a little melodramatic. "I won't be returning to the house, Ross. I'm moving back to my condo."

"Don't do that, Kit." A tremor threaded his voice. "Laura could use your company. I'm taking her home in the morning. Don't upset her by saying anything else. She needs you with her right now."

Kit's face closed up. "She has you, Ross. I'm bowing out of your lives and your marriage. I have my own life to live. A little distance will be good for all of us."

"Wait a minute!" he said in a panic-stricken voice. "I know how upset I sounded a second ago. We've been out of our minds with worry. If I said something to hurt your feelings, I didn't mean to. You know how I feel about you, Kit. How I've always felt."

Her eyes narrowed. "And how is that, Ross?"

"I'm crazy about you."

She started getting angry. "I thought you were crazy about your wife!"

"I am. Hell! You know what I mean. If you'd given me half a chance, I'd have probably asked you to marry me, but you couldn't see me at all, could you, Kit? Your father—"

"What about Daddy?"

"Nothing. Forget it."

No man could ever measure up to your father. Jarod's words exactly.

"Look—that was a long time ago. I'm in love with Laura, but you seem to need convincing that I care about you. Laura will never forgive me if she finds out I hurt you. Please, Kit. Don't do this to me. To any of us. Why can't you come home and let us be a family again?''

Finally, Ross had Kit's attention.

For a minute, she felt all the honesty he was capable of come pouring out. Deep inside she knew he wasn't the stalker.

''I care about both of you, too, and you haven't hurt me, Ross. But it's time for me to make my own way.''

''Aren't you afraid to be at the condo by yourself? I don't like it, Kit. That lunatic might start things up again.''

''I'm taking care of that problem. I'll tell you about it when I see you. Could I speak to Laura now?''

He paused. ''I'll get her, but I think I'll break the news first. She's been temperamental for months.'' His breathing became labored. ''The doctor thinks she might have been depressed for years and should get into therapy. Maybe he's right.''

Maybe, Kit conceded.

''Anyway, I don't honestly know how she'll react when she finds out you're on the phone.''

''I'm ready.''

''Does Jeremy know you're all right?''

''No. Please let me be the one to tell him, Ross.''

''Sure. But when will that be?''

''Soon.''

''Hell,'' he muttered. ''I'll get Laura.''

Kit lay back against the pillow and waited.

Odd how distanced she felt from everyone but Jarod. He was probably lying on his bed getting some much-needed rest. Only a wall separated them. She wished they were together right now, entwined in each other's arms. More than anything in the world, she wanted to make love to him, to be loved by him....

CHAPTER NINE

"KIT?" Laura's voice sounded brittle.

"Laura? How are you?"

"I can't believe it's you. Ross said you were on the phone. Why did you do it, Kit? Why did you do this to me? How could you have been so cruel?" she cried out in a shaky voice and started sobbing.

Kit's breathing grew shallow. Though she had new insight into their relationship, she still wasn't immune to her sister's accusations. "I had to do it for me, Laura. I had to separate myself from everyone or lose my mind."

"You've added ten years to my life. I almost lost the baby. Do you have any conception of the lives you've hurt? The people who've been worried sick?

"The police have lived at our house, put bugging devices on the phone, monitoring our every move. I feel like I've been in prison. Do you hear me, Kit?

"I don't care how frightened you were. You had no right to disappear like that. What could you have been thinking? Why didn't you talk to me? Why didn't you tell me you planned to run away? If you needed to leave that badly, why couldn't you have confided in your only sister about something this earthshaking? Sometimes I can't believe you *are* my sister."

A stillness fell over Kit. She straightened and held the phone a little away from her ear. The invective flowing out of Laura's mouth stunned her. As with most sisters, there'd been moments growing up when they'd been upset, but she'd never heard Laura speak like this before.

Kit was on the verge of saying she was sorry when she caught herself in time. "You're upset, Laura, and I don't blame you. I'm just thankful that you haven't miscarried. Ross says you're going home tomorrow. That's wonderful. I'll be seeing you soon and we'll have a long talk. Now isn't the time to go into all the reasons why I disappeared."

"Because nothing you say can excuse your behavior," Laura retorted. "After you saw that note in the program, couldn't you have waited for us so we could have talked about it?"

"By that time, I had no faith in the police, Laura. I—I have to hang up now."

"When am I going to see you?"

"Soon."

"What do you mean, soon? Tomorrow, next month, next year?"

Kit was aghast. "When I'm ready."

"And maybe I'll see you again when I'm ready." The line went dead.

While Kit attempted to recover from their conversation, there was a knock on the door and Jarod let himself in. He brought the tape recorder with him.

His eyes searched hers relentlessly. "If you want to talk about it, I'm here."

She sat on the side of the bed and hid her face in her hands. "I don't know what to think. She sounded like the Laura I know, but it seemed as if there was another dimension to her. Does that make sense?"

Jarod lounged back in one of the chairs. "Tell me more."

"Her anger was so intense. More than anger. It was like—"

"Rage?" he supplied.

"Yes!" she burst out. "She was in a rage. She didn't even hear me, Jarod. Any empathy or compassion or sympathy for my ordeal were missing. Naturally, I expected recrimination to a degree. But I didn't hear any of the kind of grudgingly affectionate responses I would have expected. Ross said her doctor suspects a chemical imbalance since her miscarriage. Could that account for her behavior?"

"Definitely. I know from experience that a woman's hormones and body chemistry can undergo startling changes at a time like that. I'll ask Dart if he can find out more about her doctor's opinion. How did it go with Ross?"

"He let off steam at first, but it went as well as I could have hoped for. I know he's not responsible for those notes."

Something flickered in the depths of Jarod's eyes. "Perhaps if we play the tape, you can analyze your sister's reaction and put it into some kind of perspective. It will be different this time because you're a spectator, not the participant. How do you feel about reviewing it? I'll leave the room if you prefer."

"No!" She gazed at him imploringly. "I want you to hear it. I want your opinion of Laura's reaction."

He placed the recorder next to her on the bed. "Ready?"

She nodded and started listening. There was a slight distortion that made her own voice sound a little different. In a way, it helped. Kit felt she could remain more detached.

After the segment with Ross, Jarod stopped the tape. "He's right, you know. You have changed. You sound strong, confident and very sure of yourself. Do you really feel that way, or did you have to work hard to achieve that calm, level-headed tone I heard?"

She was pensive. "I felt in control. But that's because you've managed to make me see my relationships with people more clearly. I don't feel the guilt. Because of that, I guess I don't feel as defensive."

A satisfied expression crossed his handsome face. "Good. Let's go on then." He started the tape again. Kit's heart pounded a little harder as soon as she heard Laura's voice.

The next few minutes had an air of unreality for Kit. The words that spilled forth sounded as if they came from a stranger—not her sister. Jarod's face remained impassive. When he heard the click, he shut off the tape.

"Am I right?" she urged him to answer. "Does she sound in a rage to you?"

Jarod got to his feet and looked down at Kit. "She has a lot going on inside. People with chemical imbalances can behave very differently and not be aware of it. Certainly a miscarriage is one of the greatest losses a woman can suffer. Perhaps that, plus your father's recent death, triggered something that has temporarily affected her behavior."

"My poor sister," Kit agonized.

"You have a healthy attitude, Kit, because you're not blaming yourself for what you heard. According to you, your sister has always managed to make you feel guilty. It's a habit she's brought to her adult world. It's exaggerated now because of her pregnancy and other factors."

He put his hands on his hips. "Let's play the tape once more."

Puzzled, she looked up at him. "Why?"

"Because human behavior is fascinating and we both might learn something. Let's study Ross's and Laura's patterns of conversation. Who makes the most statements? Who asks the most questions? We'll both make a list and compare notes."

"All right," she said hesitantly as he handed her some motel stationery and a pencil.

For a second time, they listened to Ross, then Laura. When the tape ended, she glanced at Jarod's paper. He'd made more notations than she had.

He rewound the tape. "What did you learn?"

"That they were both angry when the conversations started. But Ross finally calmed down and we actually talked. With Laura, it was different. She never talked. She just stayed angry.''

"Your engineer's mind hasn't let you down. Ross became reasonable.''

"Yes. I see what you mean.''

"Let's play it one more time. Jot down anything that strikes you as odd or significant.''

Kit frowned. "I don't know what more there is to discover.''

"If you're tired, we can stop.''

"It's not that,'' she reasoned honestly. She was just surprised that Jarod was so intent about it. However, she'd put her trust in him this far. If he wanted her to listen again, then she'd do it.

"Kit—it's hard to do this because both subjects are so close to you. Remaining objective is a difficult task, but the more you can detach yourself emotionally, the greater insight you will develop into their psyches.

"When you go home, you will be better equipped to handle situations if you know why they happen. Your attitude will mean everything. Attitude is ninety-nine percent of living, because we can't change people.''

"I know.'' She took a deep breath. "Play the tape again.''

She found herself listening a third time. Though she didn't know what to look for, she made a few observations.

"Go ahead.'' He inclined his head.

"Ross seemed worried that I had upset Laura. Whereas Laura didn't mention Ross once. And Ross seemed afraid of Laura. Also, Laura tried to lay a guilt trip on me by mentioning how I'd gone off without telling her. Ross tried the same thing, but then he apologized.''

Jarod stared at her through veiled eyes. ''Did you notice that you remained in character throughout both conversations?''

''Yes.''

''Would you say all of you remained in character?''

''Yes, except that I couldn't bring Laura around in the end.''

''Is that out of character?''

''Yes. I suppose so.''

''Why not this time?''

''Because she was too angry.''

''Because she was in a rage.''

''Yes.''

''Putting her physical condition aside for a moment, why do you think she was so upset? Particularly as she had the reassurance that you were all right and that you'd be coming home soon?''

Kit squirmed. ''I don't know.''

''Yes, you do, Kit. Think.''

''I made her angry.''

''How?''

''Because I didn't try to placate her.''

''Is her reaction typical?''

''You mean when things don't go her way?''

''Yes. When she can't manipulate you.''

''Manipulate me?''

"Laura has learned that if she gets mad enough, you placate. It's a device she's used since childhood to get the response she wants. You've been conditioned to give that response. Tonight you didn't respond the way she wanted. What was the result?"

"She became angry and hung up on me."

"Why?"

"Why?" Kit asked, eyeing him intently.

"Yes. Why? Do you think you intimidated her by not placating her?"

Kit shifted her legs. "Laura isn't easily intimidated by anything. I think she did it to punish me."

"Punish is an interesting word. As in, you're a naughty little girl and you have to go to bed without your supper?"

"Possibly."

"What form will her punishment take when you go home and continue to resist her threats?"

"Threats?" Kit cried out.

"Manipulative behavior, then," he offered.

"She said on the phone that it may be a long time before she wants to talk to me, let alone see me."

"Does that disturb you?"

"Well, naturally it does. But I'm not ill over it."

"Why?"

"Because Ross says the doctor believes there's a chemical explanation for her behavior, a-and because you've made me see her in a new light."

Jarod rubbed his hand absently against his chest. "And when I'm no longer around to help you reason things out, will you be strong enough to remain objective? Or do you think you'll fall back into the old patterns because it's easier on you emotionally?"

Suddenly, Kit lost interest in their game. Jarod had all but told her that when she went back to Salt Lake on Monday, she'd never see him again.

She rose to her feet, hugging her arms to her chest. Never to be with him, or hear his deep laughter... Never to talk and share like this again... The pain was too excruciating.

Wheeling around, she said, "I—I don't want to talk about this anymore if you don't mind. I'm tired and think I'll go to bed."

He, too, got up from the chair. A mask seemed to have slipped into place so she couldn't tell what he was thinking.

"I'll be next door if you need me."

Long after he'd gone, she curled up in a ball on the bed and tried to stifle her sobs in the pillows.

She couldn't have let their conversation go on any longer. For the first time since she'd known Jarod, she couldn't tell the truth.

It wasn't Laura who upset her. Jarod had helped her conquer that problem. *It was Jarod.* She loved him madly, passionately. Life made no sense without him.

She wept until her tears were spent. It was after midnight when she turned over on her back, another decision made.

Jarod would never abandon her until the person writing those notes had been caught because that was the way he was made. A caring, compassionate, professional doctor. So the only fair thing to do was go home on Monday and get it over with. He had another life, one she'd interrupted. Lucy was waiting....

But just thinking about Lucy produced more torment. Desperate at this point, Kit got up for a drink of water, then paced the floor for ten minutes.

If she were another kind of woman, if she hadn't been brought up with the values and principles instilled in her by her parents, she might have slipped over to Jarod's room and made herself available to him. For many women, one night in the arms of the man you loved would be worth it, even if he didn't love you.

Maybe Jarod would have welcomed Kit for a night's pleasure, maybe not. She knew he liked her, that there was a special bond between them. But that kiss on her forehead had had as much passion as one of her father's good-night pecks. She was only deluding herself if she tried to read anything more into it.

In the midst of her pacing, her gaze inadvertently fell on the tape recorder. She paused to pick it up from the end of the bed. Had Jarod left it by accident or on purpose?

Her eyebrows knit together. He'd been unusually persistent about listening to that tape. Almost relentless. He'd kept on probing and digging. She couldn't imagine why. Wasn't he convinced that she'd become strong enough to deal with Laura?

On impulse, she rewound the tape and started playing it again, keeping the volume down. She'd been the one to call a halt earlier. Jarod had been prepared to go on indefinitely. Again, she had to ask—why?

Flopping in the chair with her arms around her upraised knees, she listened, particularly to Laura.

Her sister didn't like the invasion of her privacy by the police and media. That was understandable. She might have lost this baby, but she was still pregnant.

Laura hated it that Kit hadn't told her about her plans to run away. That was nothing new. Kit had realized early in life that her sister liked to be in control. She was angry because Kit hadn't given her a timetable for coming home.

After weighing everything, Kit came to the conclusion that the only thing that might have justified Laura's anger was her not telling her sister about that note in the program.

Ross, on the other hand, seemed upset for different reasons. He thought she'd been kidnapped. Laura hadn't mentioned it. When Ross realized the hell they'd been through for nothing, then he got angry. He didn't mention the ballet at all.

Kit listened to the tape again. She heard herself telling Ross why she'd fled from the ballet. Because the psychopath had left his calling card.

Suddenly, her thoughts flashed back to Laura's statement about the note in the program. The hairs on her neck began to prickle.

How did Laura know about that?

How did she know anything about the placement of the note? Not from Ross! *Not from another living soul*.

An electric current sizzled through Kit's body like an exploding rocket. She leaped out of the chair, her heart knocking against her breast until she couldn't breathe.

"*Jarod*!" she cried out. "*Jarod*!" she screamed at the top of her lungs, running to the next room and pounding on the door.

Several lights went on inside some units in the motel, but Jarod ignored them and pulled her into his room.

Like a rock, he was there for her, solid and steady. She wanted to throw herself into his arms, but checked herself.

"I told you that given enough time you might solve your own case."

Kit's body shook convulsively. She looked at him as if seeing him for the first time. "How long have you known Laura was the person responsible for everything?"

He took a tentative step toward her, one hand in his back pocket. "I've suspected her from the beginning, but I didn't have proof until Dart tracked down the person giving out programs at the ballet, the person Laura bribed to give you a program with her note tucked inside."

Kit stood there with accusing eyes. Her pain went too deep for tears. "Why didn't you just come out and tell me it was Laura? Why did I have to go through all this?'' she lashed out, her breasts heaving.

Why did you make me spend all this time with you so that now I'm so in love, I'll never be the same again?

"Would you have believed me?'' he asked in a deceptively calm voice. "Would you have given me the opportunity to explain my reasons for suspecting her? Would you have worked with me, spent time with me if I had cast aspersions on your sister's character? Pointed out her flaws?

"You're like a mother lion with her cubs where Laura is concerned. Your loyalty to her is commendable, but it almost cost you your sanity. You had to stumble onto the truth by yourself. You took off the blinders with everyone but Laura.''

Kit couldn't say anything for a minute because the truth of his words pounded in her ears.

"It's all right to hate me, Kit. You wouldn't be the first patient of mine to be upset by a diagnosis. But in the end, the results outweigh the drawbacks.''

No. They don't! she cried inwardly.

She took a shaky breath, clenching her hands. "You left that recorder with me on purpose.''

He nodded. "I hoped that marvelous brain of yours would become curious enough to find out what I was after.''

I don't want you to love my marvelous brain. I want you to love me, Jarod Banning.

She turned away from him. "If I hadn't figured it out, what would you have done?''

He rubbed his lower lip with his thumb. "Nothing. You would have gone back to Salt Lake none the wiser, and we'd have carried on with our plan to catch her in the act. Which would be the most palatable to you?"

Her chin quivered. "None of it," she whispered. "None of it."

"The tape isn't hard evidence, but the ballet usher's testimony would be enough to prove Laura is the guilty party."

"*Dear God.*"

"The reason why the police didn't catch Laura before the incident at the ballet was because, as far as we can tell, she didn't use anyone else to help her plant the other notes."

Kit started to shiver and couldn't stop.

"Sit down, Kit, and catch your breath," he urged. "Your face has lost its color."

She sank into a chair, totally dazed.

"Only one thing has changed. You know the identity of your stalker. Now her doctor can be informed of what she's done so he can help her. But you mustn't be the one to confront her at this stage. We have no way of knowing how she'll react when she realizes you know she's the one responsible for the notes."

Once again Kit hid her face in her hands. The nightmare seemed to go on and on.

"She's going to get the help she needs."

Kit felt him walk over to her and get down on his haunches. In the next instance, he pulled her hands away from her face and held on to them.

"The sooner she's forced to deal with this, the better it will be for everyone, especially the baby."

She felt the tears start once more.

"I know you love Laura. That's why I'm proposing a plan that I think will be the best for all of you."

He was making sense. He always made sense, but Kit was too drained to think. She couldn't comprehend that Laura had masterminded the whole scheme. It didn't seem in the realm of possibility, yet Kit had undeniable proof on that tape.

The pressure on her hands intensified, but she felt cocooned in cotton wool, as if everything were far away and removed. He said her name again.

"W-what's your plan?" she finally asked, responding to his prodding and wiping her eyes like a little child.

"With help, your sister can resolve her childhood feelings about you, and once her chemical imbalance is under control, you won't see that irrational side of her any more. Especially with another baby on the way."

"You think she'll be all right?" she cried out, her heart in her eyes.

"I do. But when she's feeling better, physically and emotionally, she's going to be full of remorse. Let's give her some time to heal."

Kit held her breath. "For how long?"

"That will be up to her doctor."

"Do you mean *totally* out of sight, that I shouldn't go back to Salt Lake?"

"Why don't you let him decide that?"

She rubbed her throbbing temples and got to her feet. "Jeremy will be furious."

"On the contrary, he thinks you walk on water. Your job is secure whenever you decide to go back to work."

"I suppose I could go away. I have some cousins in Colorado." How horrible it sounded.

"Why go anywhere? Why not stay at the ranch? My offer still stands."

Don't do this to me, Jarod. Please, don't.

"That's your sister-in-law's home," she fired at him. "I wouldn't dream of imposing on her like that."

One brow quirked. "She won't be at the ranch. Her parents live in Sacramento. They've been begging her to bring the children and stay with them for a while. Lucy has decided to go."

For how long? Until you're sure she no longer sees Grayson in your eyes and smile? Kit lamented inwardly.

"If it's any comfort, I'll be in Salt Lake ninety percent of the time. You'll have the ranch to yourself. We can hook up the computer in my study to yours at Stragi-Corp. You can work on all the projects Jeremy gives you without having to set foot outside Heber."

She started shaking her head. "That's very kind of you, but I couldn't possibly accept."

Afraid she'd burst into another paroxysm of tears, she left his room and made a dash for her own. But she wasn't fast enough to lock the door on him.

His hard-muscled physique filled the opening. "If you're worried about money, you can pay me rent and everything else you've already figured out you owe me. I took a peek at your lists. Anytime you decide to become a C.P.A., let me know. I could use a good one."

Why was he keeping this up? The truth was, there was no more excuse to live with Jarod.

A pain more devastating than learning about Laura's illness lanced through her body. She would have to leave for somewhere else first thing in the morning. It didn't matter that Lucy might be going to California. It was only a temporary measure. Then she'd be back. Kit would never be able to handle it.

With her emotions boiling over, she reached for the wig and glasses and tossed them into the wastebasket.

"My sentiments exactly," Jarod murmured. "I much preferred you in that fetching swan outfit. At least now we know it will be kept in the family."

Kit couldn't take any more and wheeled around, her eyes bright with unshed tears. "It's over, Jarod. You've saved my life and helped me solve all my problems. Why do you continue to be so nice to me?

"You've surpassed all expectations of the Hippocratic oath," she went on. "You've done more than any person would ever do to help a neighbor in distress. I would give anything on earth to be able to repay you for what you've done for me."

"Do you mean that?" he demanded, his eyes blazing a hot blue.

Kit felt a strange pain in her heart. "How could you even ask?"

"Then accept my hospitality and we'll consider all debts paid in full."

She put a hand to her throat. "I don't understand."

"It's a case of 'Physician, heal thyself.'"

"What do you mean?"

"My wife gave up when everything looked its darkest. She felt she had nothing to offer, so she asked nothing of me in return. She robbed me of giving her what was in my capacity to give. I've lived with that pain and that burden too many years.

"Then this wounded swan came into my clinic. When everything looked its darkest to her, she entrusted me with her soul and let me give what I was capable of giving. She'll never know what she did for me.

"Don't deprive me of something that is healing *my* soul. You need help until your sister gets back to normal. And I still need to help you. But like my wife, you must make the choice. Let me know in the morning."

CHAPTER TEN

KIT loved driving the Jeep. It had belonged to Jarod's brother and got little use. Jarod insisted she run around in it for as long as she stayed in the mountains.

Carrying much-needed supplies for the office, she pulled up to the ranch house and carefully made her way inside. An unseasonal February thaw had melted a lot of the snow, making things messy. She hastily pulled off her boots, hating to get any mud on the floors.

Jarod's bedroom and study were her favorite rooms in the house because they both had huge picture windows that faced the snowcapped mountains and gave a breathtaking view.

In the past five weeks, she'd turned his study into a miniengineering lab. Since the matter of her disappearance had been settled, an elated Jeremy had come up once a week, ostensibly to discuss Stragi-Corp's latest project.

But when he started staying most of the day and suggested they take a drive over to Park City for dinner, Kit had to call a halt. One of the many things she'd learned from living with Jarod during that incredible first week was to be honest and communicate that honesty before anything could be misconstrued.

In a frank conversation, she told Jeremy she liked him as a boss, nothing more. She also believed that he was probably in love with his ex-wife and ought to do something about it.

At first, Jeremy went quiet, but then he admitted he still had some unresolved feelings. Kit encouraged him to explore those feelings and he said he'd think about it. Most importantly, he made her a promise to keep their relationship on a purely friendly basis, which came as a great relief.

Another visitor had begun making the ranch a home away from home. Ross either came up or called every day. With Laura responding so favorably to treatment, he wanted to talk about it, and he wanted to reassure Kit.

It seemed that when the doctor told Laura he knew about the notes she'd planted to frighten her sister, Laura broke down, absolutely crushed that she'd ever been capable of such cruelty. At that point, a breakthrough was achieved and he was able to start treating her.

He also suggested that Laura and Ross go to marriage counseling together. To Kit's surprise, they were both doing just that. She could tell it was making a difference when Ross revealed that he'd decided not to run for governor and had pulled out of the race. His wife and child-to-be needed to come first.

The best news was that the doctor expected Laura to make a full recovery and Ross was ecstatic. For the first time in their relationship, Kit started to feel closer to him and experienced a sense of family, of pulling together.

Perhaps the most surprising outcome of her disappearance was the show of love from friends and acquaintances. She received an outpouring of cards, letters and phone calls expressing their sympathy for her ordeal.

With Dart's help, the official word had gone out to the media that there'd been a stalking situation that had forced Kit to go into hiding. Fortunately, the stalker, who would remain unidentified, had been caught and the case was officially closed. Everything had been handled so discreetly, no one would ever know about Laura's involvement.

Kit asked Dart for a bill so she could pay him, but he just smiled and said that he'd had so much fun, it wouldn't seem right. But he did accept her dinner invitation, which included his wife and Jarod. The four of them spent a lovely evening together with Jarod being his charming, congenial self. It crushed her to think there'd never be another night like it.

Though Kit was alone most of the time, she didn't feel lonely or uneasy. Lucy's cleaning woman made her weekly rounds so that the house remained immaculately cared for. On any given day, the ranch hands would stop by for one thing or another, probably at Jarod's suggestion.

Jarod . . . The one person Kit craved most to see in the world.

He'd been up twice since the dinner, but only for the day that he spent at his office keeping appointments and clearing things up.

On both occasions, she hadn't known he was in town until he'd come by the house around six in the evening to drop off tapes for her to transcribe. It devastated her to learn that he'd been less than two miles away and hadn't mentioned that he was in town, hadn't suggested that she come into the office to help.

She found it was getting harder and harder to hide her pain around him. She wished he wouldn't ask her questions about how she was feeling, how things were going, forcing her to come up with a cheerful response when her heart was breaking.

Not once did he indicate that he needed her or missed her company. Those halcyon days at his clinic in Salt Lake might never have been. That amazing rapport she'd always felt with him seemed to have evaporated. It proved to Kit once and for all that although he was getting pleasure out of helping her, Lucy held his heart. No doubt he was biding his time until her return from California.

Work was no longer the panacea for Kit's heartache. Before she'd met Jarod, she could get started on a project and lose herself in it for twelve, fourteen hours at a time.

Now, right in the middle of a graph, her eyes would wander around his study, taking in his books and pictures, the little meomentos he treasured. She'd imagine herself his wife. From there, her thoughts would grow so intimate she'd blush and try to get back on track.

Praying that today would be different, that she could put Jarod out of her mind for a few hours at least, Kit started loading the new paper in her printer.

When the phone rang, she stopped long enough to answer it.

"High Rustler Ranch."

"*Kit*?"

"*Laura!*"

Suddenly, Kit could hear her sister sobbing, and it took a minute or more before she got herself under control. "I—I don't blame you if you never want to talk to me again."

"Don't say that, Laura. I love you."

"The doctor said my hormones went crazy when I miscarried, but I can't believe I could have done that to you. I can only pray that one day you'll be able to forgive me."

Now it was Kit who couldn't stop the flow of tears. "I already have. You poor thing. You've been through so much."

"No. You're the one who's suffered. I'll spend the rest of my life trying to make it up to you. I do love you, Kit. More than you'll ever know. But I've always been jealous of you. I'm so ashamed, and so sorry."

"Don't be. It's over. I just want you to be happy, Laura."

"I don't think I've ever been happier where Ross and the baby are concerned. But when I look back on what I did . . ." She sounded devastated, and it removed any lingering pain from Kit's heart.

"You weren't yourself. You couldn't help it. Let's not think about it anymore."

"Then come home. Please, Kit. Come home. I want us to be friends. Real friends. Forever. I need to hug you." She broke down sobbing again.

In a choked-up voice, Kit cried, "I'm coming, Laura. I'll see you very soon." She hung up the phone.

Though Kit was overjoyed by Laura's recovery, her body had started to tremble in abject misery. Jarod had told her she could stay at the ranch until Laura had improved. That day had come. . . .

It was over. *Everything was over*. Tears gushed down her wan face, drenching her T-shirt. Before she did something insane like running away again, she picked up the receiver and phoned Ross at the law firm. Before the day was out, she wanted to be gone from the ranch, from Jarod's life.

Once she'd made that phone call, she sat down and composed a letter to Jarod, explaining that the crisis with Laura had passed, that she was moving back to her condo.

After thanking him for everything, she came to the end and wrote, "Now all debts are paid in full. May you find the true happiness in life that you more than anyone else in this world so richly deserve. Kit."

She enclosed a check to cover the rent of the clinic and ranch house, plus the multitude of things he'd bought her.

Since Jarod stayed in constant touch with his foreman, Kit would leave the letter, plus the keys to the house and Jeep, with him.

With the important things accomplished, she immediately started to pack everything she'd need to transport back to Salt Lake. Later in the day, when she walked out the door with Ross, she didn't want to leave one reminder that she'd ever occupied the premises. Certainly not the costume.

"Hey, Kit? There's someone at the front desk who wants to talk to you."

Kit was knee-deep in a waste-management report for Jeremy, which had to be on his desk by the end of lunch. Still typing into the computer, she muttered, "Whoever it is, I can't come right now, Arnie."

"She said her name is Lucy Banning."

The shock of hearing Lucy's name caused Kit to press the wrong key, thereby deleting the portion she'd been working on since seven that morning.

She jumped up and headed for the door of her office. "Arnie, run and get Lori. She's the only computer technician around here and will know exactly how to get inside that thing and retrieve what I've just lost. Jeremy needs it right away."

"I think she and Bill left for lunch."

"Then grab her as soon as she gets back. Do that for me and I'll edit that statics paper of yours."

"You're on!"

Every nerve electrified, Kit hurried through the maze of corridors to the reception area of the Stragi-Corp building.

Dressed in a pullover and jeans, her usual attire at work, Kit felt intimidated the second she laid eyes on Lucy, who sported a beautiful California suntan and had achieved a chic elegance in a coffee-colored three-piece suit of raw silk. Being in the sun had brought out the white-gold highlights of her hair, which she'd had cut in a youthful style.

She was a far different creature than the shattered woman who'd left Heber with her children over two months ago.

Kit thought she looked beautiful and more contented. Obviously Jarod's doing. Any woman lucky enough, blessed enough, to be loved by him *would* be transformed.

What earthly reason would Lucy have for coming here?

Since Kit's flight from Heber, it had taken three hellish weeks for her to get back to some semblance of normality. Between emotional visits to her sister, who was so filled with remorse it broke Kit's heart, plus adjusting to the hectic pace at the office, she was barely starting to cope.

In all that time, there'd been no word from Jarod. She knew that the foreman would have given her letter to him. So it meant that Jarod had agreed with her, that their debts had canceled each other out. End of story....

"Hello, Kit." Lucy took the initiative. "I'm sure you're surprised to see me, and I've probably come at a bad time. But I was afraid you might not take my phone call."

"Of course I would have. It looks like you've had a marvelous trip. How are the children?"

"They're fine. I wish I could say the same for Jarod."

"*What's wrong with Jarod*?" she blurted in panic.

"Probably the same thing that's wrong with you."

Stunned by Lucy's comment, Kit didn't know what to say.

"My brother-in-law is painfully in love with you. It was written all over him the day the children and I burst in on the two of you."

"What...?" Kit couldn't take it in.

"If I hadn't fallen apart so completely after Grayson died, you'd most likely be Mrs. Jarod Banning by now."

"But—"

"You don't need to pretend with me, Kit," she broke in. "I know what it's like to fall in love with a Banning. You show all the signs. I'm warning you that it's fatal.

"But I met someone in California who made me realize I still have the rest of my life to get through. My memories of Grayson won't be enough, and Jarod isn't Grayson, although he has many of the traits I loved in my husband.

"What I'm trying to say is, I came here to apologize for the way I treated you. The children are already crazy about you. If we're going to be sisters-in-law, I'd like us to be friends."

Kit still couldn't take it in. Her heart leaped to her throat. "I—I'd like that, too, but you're wrong about Jarod's feelings for me. I haven't heard from him since I left the ranch."

"Well—you didn't leave him much to go on. Last night when I saw him, he was muttering something about your father, and not forcing you, and your not wanting one damn thing from him. But of course, he'd had too much to drink so I couldn't make out any more than that. Do you have any idea what he meant?''

"Yes!" Kit cried out in agony. "But that's crazy. I love him and—"

"Then I guess you'd better tell him that," Lucy interrupted. "You might as well know something right now. Doctors make the worst patients and they are notorious for being able to diagnose everyone else's problems but their own."

The two women smiled at each other. Then Lucy leaned forward and patted Kit's arm, her expression sobering.

"Jarod has suffered two painful losses with the death of his wife and Grayson. But I think if he lost you, it could do permanent damage."

When the warning sank in, Kit's body started to tremble uncontrollably. "Lucy..." She tried to convey her feelings, but couldn't seem to form the words. In a spontaneous gesture of affection, she reached out for the older woman.

The clock inside the taxi said ten forty-five. Kit strained to see out the back window without the driver noticing. She pretended to be in great pain from a fall after dancing at the ballet.

One lonely light shone from Jarod's room above the clinic. She hoped that meant he was home!

"You're sure this is a doctor's office?" the man asked.

"Yes. I've been here before. He takes cases after hours and doesn't charge very much. If you'll just help me up the stairs, please."

"Sure."

Within minutes, the fortyish taxi driver had rung the buzzer. Kit leaned all her weight against him, and with little moaning sounds rested her head on his thin shoulder.

The second the door opened, Kit lunged for Jarod, throwing her arms around his sweatered chest. "Dr. Banning! I'm so thankful you're here. Help me. I feel faint."

It was the truth. But it was because she felt herself being crushed against Jarod's strong, hard body, where his heart was thudding as fast and furiously as hers.

"I'll pay you after I take care of her," Jarod told the driver.

"That's okay. This one's on me."

The door closed and Jarod activated the electronic lock. It was the sound she'd been waiting for because it meant they were alone, exactly where she wanted to be.

He took one look at her face. "*Dear God. Kit!* It *is* you," he cried in a fierce whisper, his arms going completely around her. "What the devil are you doing in that costume?"

She didn't want to answer him. Not yet. Instead, she sagged in his arms, her head lolling against his shoulder to make herself into a dead weight.

After an anxious imprecation, he picked her up and practically ran to the first examining room, where he laid her down. But this time, all signs of the methodical internist had disappeared.

On a ragged breath, he cried her name once more, feeling for the pulse in her neck, running his trembling hands down the length of her body enveloped in the cape.

"Jarod..." she called softly.

"Thank God you're conscious. What's wrong, darling? Tell me!"

Darling. What a beautiful word. "You're such a wonderful doctor, I'm surprised you don't know what's the matter."

His hands moved with frantic speed to the headdress, which he carefully removed. With a sense of déjà vu, he slid his fingers into her black curls, searching for evidence of a lump. With each caress, hot little flames of desire ignited every nerve in her body.

"You're looking in the wrong place."

His color receded as he opened the cape, exposing her limbs to his gaze. Through veiled eyes, she watched the various expressions play across his hard-boned features as he began to examine her with a concern that smote her heart.

For so many weeks she'd tried to imagine his hands on her body. The sensation was exquisite. She simply couldn't hold out any longer.

With a boldness she didn't know herself capable of, she lifted her arms and caught him around his neck, neatly trapping him. "I'm surprised at you, Dr. Banning," she said in a husky voice. "You're the brilliant diagnostician with everyone else. How come you haven't recognized the full-blown symptoms of a woman in love?"

The blue eyes that had been concentrating during his examination darkened in intensity. "*Kit...*"

Everything she ever wanted to hear come out of Jarod was there when he cried her name.

"I need treatment, darling. I need it now," she murmured against his lips. "Don't make me wait another sec—"

Suddenly, his mouth took hers by storm, smothering any other words. Kit had been wanting this for so long her lips opened eagerly to the hungry demand of his, compelling him to give everything while she tried desperately to merge with him.

No longer in a game of pretense, the little moans escaping her throat came out of their own volition. Every touch, every caress, sent her into an ecstatic spiral compelling her to cling to him.

"*Jarod*!" She cried his name over and over again. "I love you," she whispered between each feverish kiss. "If you only had any idea how much."

"Let's find out, shall we?" he said against her mouth, before lifting her off the table so their bodies could fuse, as well.

Kit had never been in love before. She wasn't prepared for this cataclysm of emotion that engulfed the senses and the soul, uniting them in one great passion. All she knew was that Jarod was holding her, kissing her as if she were the only thing that mattered in the universe. Her joy was so great, she needed to go on giving and never stop.

"I wanted to do this to you that first night," he confessed, raining kisses on her neck and shoulders. "I was in love with you the moment I looked into your haunted green eyes. I wanted to be the one to take that fear away."

"You *were* the one," she whispered, kissing the side of his face, savoring the taste of his hair and skin.

"Every part of that medical exam was pure torture for me. I was supposed to be a doctor with healing on my mind. Instead, all I could think about was how it would feel to have your beautiful body wrapped around mine.

"I almost broke the rules and took you to bed with me where you would be safe, where I could kiss your delectable mouth whenever I wanted." A tremor shook his powerful frame.

"Why didn't you?" she cried out.

"Don't ask me that," he groaned, running his hands over her back and hips, molding her to him with increasing urgency.

"Darling—" she cupped his face in her hands "—it's my turn for confession. That first night when you undid my cape and looked down at me, I would have let you do anything you wanted to me. I never wanted that examination to stop."

"*Kit* . . ." He sounded shocked.

"It's true. I couldn't believe I could feel like that. Here I'd been so terrified, I had run away. And in the next instant, there was this incredible man standing over me, touching my skin and hair, gentling me, arousing me unknowingly until my body became one aching mass of need. It's never gone away."

He breathed in sharply. "I've been living with those same needs until I've almost gone out of my mind. That day when I found you crying on my bed . . . Kit . . ." His voice throbbed. "I didn't stop to think. I just pulled you into my arms. I couldn't help myself.''

It was her turn to gasp. ''I came within an inch of kissing you right then, Jarod. And that night at the motel? You'll never know how hard I had to fight not to knock on your door and beg you to love me, even though I thought it was Lucy you wanted.''

At the mention of his sister-in-law, his hands stilled on her upper arms. He stared into Kit's eyes, willing her to believe him. ''I never wanted Lucy.''

''I know that now. And after this afternoon, I've no concerns about the kind of feeling she has for you, either.''

His brows met in a frown. ''What happened?''

''She came to see me at work, to apologize. In essence, she felt it was important for us to get along since we were going to be sisters-in-law.''

Once again, Kit found herself crushed in his arms. ''Thank God she went to California and got her head on straight. If it hadn't been for Lucy—''

''Don't think about it anymore, darling. We're together now. It's all I care about.''

''Marry me, Kit.''

''As soon as possible.''

''Tomorrow,'' he begged, burying his face in her curls.

Kit let out an ecstatic sigh. ''I'm so thankful you said that. I don't want to wait.''

''What about the big wedding your father would have wanted for you?''

"Jarod—if both of us had parents who were still alive, if Lucy and Laura were at another stage in their lives, you and I wouldn't think of doing anything else. But right now, for the sake of our loved ones, a quiet ceremony for the two of us is all I desire." She barely got the words out before he was kissing her again.

And a few minutes later came a proposal. "How would you feel about being married in our family church?"

"Do you even have to ask?"

"I'll phone the pastor first thing in the morning. We'll pick up a license and drive to Heber."

"I can't believe this is happening to me." She shivered with excitement.

"Kit—there's something else we need to discuss." He sounded serious.

"If it's about children, I think we should get started as soon as possible." She saw Jarod swallow hard and knew how much her words meant to him. "You'll make such a wonderful father that I want at least four."

"But what about your work?"

"With that computer hookup at the ranch, I found it possible to do the bulk of my project away from the office. I can set up the same system here. Jeremy is willing to make concessions."

"He's in love with you," Jarod said quietly.

"He thought he was, but that's all been straightened out. He knows how I feel about you."

Jarod took the hand he'd been squeezing and kissed her palm. "How about staying here during the week, going back to the ranch on weekends?"

She gave him the benefit of a full-bodied smile. "It's perfect, but what about Lucy?"

"She met a man in California."

"I gathered."

"Something tells me she's going to be spending more and more time down there."

"He must be pretty remarkable to have made an impact on your sister-in-law in this short a time. As she told me, once you fall for a Banning, it's fatal."

His mouth curved upward. "Is that so?"

"You know so," she admitted, hiding her face in his neck.

"In that case, I'm going to suggest that you sleep down here tonight, my wounded swan."

"*What*?"

"That's right. No matter where he is, I have this feeling your father is looking on and I want his approval."

"But, darling—" she protested.

"What's one more night when we'll have the rest of our lives to be together?"

She couldn't believe it. "You're serious!"

"Kit—" he said her name rather emotionally "—I'm not taking any chances where you're concerned. I want to do everything right."

Jarod Banning would always be an honorable man. That's why she adored him.

"Well," she said, affecting a wobble in her voice, "if that's what you want, then I suggest you go upstairs now." She broke away from him and climbed back on the examining table, pulling the sheet over her. "Do you mind extinguishing the light?"

He looked like a man who'd just gone into shock. With a satisfied smile, she turned away from him. Seconds later, the room was shrouded in darkness.

When it became clear that he wasn't going to leave the room, she murmured, "You can give me a good-night kiss if you'd like."

"Where?"

She hid another smile in her arm. "On my forehead."

"I'd better not," he grated.

"What are you afraid of, Doctor?"

"You *know* what!"

She stretched luxuriously. "Then come on over here and let me give you one."

"Don't do this to me, Kit."

"Are we having our second fight?"

There was a pause. "I'm not sure what we're having."

"In that case, I think there's just enough room for you to climb up here with me. I wouldn't dream of asking you to do anything but hold me. In fact, if you tried anything else, we'd fall off. How about it?"

"You really think it will hold both of us?"

"You mean you haven't already tested your own equipment?"

A low chuckle came out of him. The most beautiful sound she'd ever heard. "I was waiting for you."

"Well, I'm here."

"I know," he said, his voice throbbing.

"I'll count to ten if that will help."

"It won't."

"One...two...three..."

She heard him suck in his breath.

"Four...five...six..."

His frustration reached out to her like a living thing.

"Seven...eight...nine..."

A long pause.

"Ten."

"Dammit, Kit..."

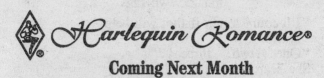

Coming Next Month

#3423 MARRYING THE BOSS! Leigh Michaels
All Keir Saunders was interested in was making money, and so when he needed a wife to complete a business deal, it seemed easiest to buy one! His secretary, Jessica, was the logical candidate. And though she was certain matrimony wasn't in her job description—how could she refuse a man like Keir?

#3424 A SIMPLE TEXAS WEDDING Ruth Jean Dale
It began simply enough when Trace Morgan hired Hope to organize his sister's engagement party…. But Trace didn't want the wedding to go ahead. And he certainly didn't want to fall in love with the hired help!

#3425 REBEL IN DISGUISE Lucy Gordon
Holding Out for a Hero
Jane was a cool, calm and collected bank manager. Gil Wakeham was a rebel. But Jane had accepted his offer of adventure—a summer spent with Gil and his adorable basset hound, Perry. The dog had stolen her sandwiches. Was Gil about to steal her heart?

#3426 SOMETHING OLD, SOMETHING NEW Catherine Leigh
Hitched!
Lily Alexander's husband, Saige, had been missing—presumed dead—for seven long years when he walked back into her life! And though Lily was overjoyed to see him, the timing was awkward, to say the least. Lily's wedding to her new fiancé was imminent! But Lily could hardly marry placid lawyer Randall when her sexy rancher husband refused to let her go!

AVAILABLE THIS MONTH:

#3419 KIT AND THE COWBOY
Rebecca Winters

#3420 EARTHBOUND ANGEL
Catherine George

#3421 TEMPORARY TEXAN
Heather Allison

#3422 DESPERATELY SEEK-ING ANNIE
Patricia Knoll

Harlequin Romance ®

brings you

How the West was Wooed!

We've rounded up twelve of our most popular authors, and the result is a whole year of romance, Western style. Every month we'll be bringing you a spirited, independent woman whose heart is about to be lassoed by a rugged, handsome, one-hundred-percent cowboy! Watch for...

- September: #3426 *SOMETHING OLD, SOMETHING NEW—*
  Catherine Leigh

- October: #3428 *WYOMING WEDDING—*
  Barbara McMahon

- November: #3432 *THE COWBOY WANTS A WIFE—*
  Susan Fox

- December: #3437 *A CHRISTMAS WEDDING—*
  Jeanne Allan

Available wherever Harlequin books are sold.

Look us up on-line at: http://www.romance.net

HITCH-8

brings you

Some men are worth waiting for!

Every month for a whole year Harlequin Romance will be bringing you some of the world's most eligible men in our special **Holding Out for a Hero** miniseries. They're handsome, they're charming but, best of all, they're single! Twelve lucky women are about to discover that finding Mr. Right is not a problem—it's holding on to him!

In September watch for:

#3425 *REBEL IN DISGUISE*
by Lucy Gordon

Available wherever Harlequin books are sold.

HOFH-9